SOME FREAKS

ALSO BY DAVID MAMET

FOR CHILDREN
The Owl, with Lindsay Crouse
Warm and Cold, with drawings by Donald Sultan

SCREENPLAYS
The Verdict
The Postman Always Rings Twice (1980)
The Untouchables
House of Games
We're No Angels (1989)
Things Change (with Shel Silverstein)
Homocide

PLAYS
American Buffalo
Edmond
Glengarry Glen Ross
Goldberg Street: Short Plays and Monologues
Lakeboat
A Life in the Theater
Reunion and *Dark Pony*
Sexual Perversity in Chicago and *The Duck Variations*
The Shawl and *Prairie du Chien*
The Water Engine and *Mr. Happiness*
The Woods
Speed-The-Plow

ESSAYS
Writing in Restaurants

POETRY
The Blood Chit

SOME FREAKS

DAVID MAMET

VIKING

VIKING
Published by the Penguin Group
Viking Penguin, a division of Penguin Books USA Inc.,
40 West 23rd Street, New York, New York 10010, U.S.A.
Penguin Books Ltd, 27 Wrights Lane, London W8 5TZ, England
Penguin Books Australia Ltd, Ringwood, Victoria, Australia
Penguin Books Canada Ltd, 2801 John Street, Markham, Ontario, Canada L3R 1B4
Penguin Books (N.Z.) Ltd, 182–190 Wairau Road, Auckland 10, New Zealand

Penguin Books Ltd, Registered Offices:
Harmondsworth, Middlesex, England

First published in 1989 by Viking Penguin,
a division of Penguin Books USA Inc.

1 3 5 7 9 10 8 6 4 2

"The Decoration of Jewish Houses" first appeared in *Penthouse*;
"A Plain Brown Wrapper" in *Tikkun*; "Women" in *New York Woman*;
"Conventional Warfare" in *Esquire*; "The Laurel Crown" as
"In Losing, a Boxer Won" in *The New York Times*; "Stanislavsky
and the Bearer Bonds" in *Lincoln Center Theatre Company
Magazine*; "A Party for Mickey Mouse" and "In the Company of Men"
in *Playboy*; "Film is a Collaborative Business" in *American
Film Magazine*; "Practical Pistol Competition" in *Sports
Illustrated*; "Encased by Technology" in *Interview*; and
"Kryptonite" in *Boston Review*. A *Practical Handbook
for the Actor* by Melissa Bruder, et al., with
an introduction by Mr. Mamet is
published by Vintage Books.

LIBRARY OF CONGRESS CATALOGING IN PUBLICATION DATA
Mamet, David.
Some freaks / David Mamet.
p.   cm.
ISBN 0–670–82933–1
I. Title.
PS3563.A4345S62   1989
814'.54—dc20   88–40650

Printed in the United States of America
Set in Electra
Designed by Michael Ian Kaye

This book is dedicated
to Lindsay Crouse

ACKNOWLEDGMENTS

I would like to thank
my editor, Dawn Seferian,
and my assistant, Catherine Shaddix,
for their help with and enthusiasm
for this book.

CONTENTS

SLAVYANSKY BAZAAR

AN INTRODUCTION

In June, Eighteen Ninety-Seven, Constantin Stanislavsky and Vladimir Nemirovich-Danchenko, two gifted theatrical amateurs, met over coffee at the Moscow emporium Slavyansky Bazaar. They talked for eighteen hours, and found their views on life, on Theater, on Art complementary in the correct places and identical in the right places. They formed a marriage which gave birth to the Moscow Art Theatre, a home to classics and an inspiration to the new writers of their day.

The name Slavyansky Bazaar always was a talisman to me. It symbolized the Place Where Three Roads Meet, the mystic Conjunction of Opposites into the Whole, the possibility of True Love; and, on a less abstract plane, the gratification of the desire for ease, comfort, and companionship.

There, at the Slavyansky Bazaar, it seemed to me, were

all the good things in life. There was good food, good conversation, alcohol and tobacco, the joy of mutual discovery,
the feeling that the universe had a plan for one, and that one
was setting about on that marvelous adventure filled with
both the virile certainty of risk and danger, and the unspeak-
able comfort of ordination.

"Yes," the men said to each other. "Yes. Isn't life like
that . . . ?" And I held that picture as a beautiful dream, and
have been privileged to partake of it from time to time.

I hope you enjoy these essays.

SOME FREAKS

SOME FREAKS

A TALK TO THE SIGNET SOCIETY,

HARVARD UNIVERSITY,

DECEMBER 11, 1988

It is traditional to dissuade those planning to pursue a career in the Fine Arts by pointing out to them how much more secure are positions in other pursuits.

These other pursuits, it occurs to me after a score of years as a writer, have the reputation of being and, in fact, *are* more secure because work in them is not judged by utility; and, in fact, the pursuits themselves are capable of absorbing any number of apprentices because they have little or no final utility; and, so, unlike a career in the Fine Arts, the public can never be surfeited by either an overabundance of practitioners, or an overabundance of unqualified practitioners. These professions are, in the words, I believe, of Mr. Veblen, a "conspiracy against the Laity." So, of course they are more secure, as there is one born every minute.

But the law of life is to do evil and good, to eat and be eaten, and the most supposedly innocuous good is, perhaps, also and occasionally violence in disguise.

What does it mean to be a member of the intelligentsia? It occurred to me one day that it is something akin to being the germ of a virus; that the intelligentsia, we "fops," are driven to seek out, to explore, to endorse, to, finally, be the first exploiters of certain aspects of the material world, that we, in our quality of avatars of fashion, are the first news of the co-option of the theretofore natural.

Which of us has not seen, heard of, and dreamt of emulating that artist, painter, writer, whatever, who quit the city and enjoyed the wild; who found rapture in the contemplation of that which the natives took for granted: beautiful views, clean water, deep woods, clear beaches, unspoiled native honesty or wit?

Well, we went there, and we *did* enjoy it, and we either wrote or painted it, or told our friends, or were discovered by those who trailed in the wake of free spirits like ourselves, so that all that remained of that beach, woods, or indigenous accent was just our depiction of it.

It was bound to happen anyway, of course, but it occurred to me that we were the disease; first speaking of that New Thing which, having been noticed, must, then, become Old.

We could not *stop* ourselves from doing it, from renovating that old house, that old Factory District, that old Basket; and, so, set fashion, and consigned the Timeless to the Round of Time, which is to say, to Death.

But at least we weren't Working in an Office All Day Long. No, we were working in an office all day long, and then carrying that office home with us in our heads for the evening and into the night, and driving our families crazy with the dreariness of our concerns for the hidden, for the exquisite. Who did we think we were?

And how useful was it, finally—as much as we, full of pride, looked at those who toiled and spun to no effect or purpose whatever other than the accumulation of Gold, or Status, or Power, or something Chimerical and Useless— when compared to the thrill we artists felt in our discoveries, or in the Populace's discovery of us. As Mr. Ginsberg wrote, "Businessmen are Serious, Politicians are Serious, every- body's serious but *Me* . . ." And so we turned to anyone who suggested that our "work" was merely a toy, and the flywheel of a great society spinning off excess steam, and weren't we *précieux*, children that we were, to assume that our work had a use. . . .

Though, of course, none of us did it because it had a use, we did it because we had an idea. We did it because, like the businessman, like the developer, we couldn't help our- selves.

Sometimes an individual is thrown up *who does not fit the norm*. One reads of the Indians of the Plains. And their magnificent society. Among the warrior race, a young boy, subject to visions, incapable of assimilating, of taking up the major burdens of the culture, of being a Man in the Culture, if you will, was given the option of becoming a Man by another, by a more solitary route, as a seer, or a sage, or Medicine Man, and so was exempted from the daily task of his brethren, and afforded a certain living, and a position in the society. And that Individual and Society as a whole benefited.

They benefited, perhaps, from his visions, and they benefited, perhaps most importantly, from the endorsement of the notion that *all* people born into the society are precious. What Is Worthwhile in a Society? I suppose it depends on how close, in time or space, one is to the phenomenon in question. Finally, pursuits, places, and people are made romantic, which is to say, irresistible, and are made to seem important in order to attract us to them as part of a plan *beyond the plan of reason.*

I was always confused by the verse "Consider the Lilies of the Field, . . . they neither toil nor spin; and yet I say unto you that even Solomon in All his Glory, was not arrayed like one of these."

And, over the years, when I would hear or think of that verse, it would seem to me specious—an indictment of *labor*, and *talent*, or perhaps, of the conjunction of the two, or of "fortune." And finally, the verse made no sense to me. It seemed to me "weak," and in praise of weakness.

I had not thought of that phrase for some time, I'd passed my fortieth year, and it came to my mind in conjunction with these thoughts, and I understood it for the first time. I had changed since last I thought of it, and I said, "Of *course*, it *is* an indictment—a gentle indictment of the prideful love of labor or talent, for that pride neglects what, to the author of that phrase, is obvious, that both that labor and that talent, that ambition and that reward, are gifts of God."

That the creation of these differing professions, these differing pursuits, different levels of achievement, of the chaos of competition, this, as in the arts, aesthetic Darwinism, taken to its logical extreme, becomes the opposite of the random view.

All professions, achievements, impulses, are thrown up to compete, to strive, to an end which is *not* chance, but is the effect of some Universal Will; and, to that end, all these efforts, of Solomon *and* the lilies of the field, are equal. It is not *given* us to know the worth of our impulses, or of our acts. To some, and, in some times, the acts the wisest have held to be the best are otherwise seen as heinous.

We are all held in the sway of a superior intelligence, and it is in the interests of that power that each of us finds his or her pursuits compelling.

It is in the interest of the Whole, and, I think, in the pursuits of something beyond the whole, that some are driven to pursue the arts, that some are driven to pursue power, or wealth, or solitude, or death.

I always felt proud, and not a little arrogant, that I was one of those freaks privileged to live in the world of the Arts. As I become older, I feel still happy, and quite privileged to be working in an area where I am happy; but I am, I hope, a bit less proud, and, increasingly, awed by the way the universe has been thoughtfully construed even to include a freak like me.

This is not to say I feel that I am devoid of talent, or that my work is devoid of worth; but that my *profession* of artistic vision arose, I think, not so much to express whatever "individual" ideas I may have had or may have, but, rather, to accommodate and embrace a deviant personality which was not going to be employed elsewhere. *Much* like the growth of the computer, and computer-run business, *coincidentally* in time to accommodate a burgeoning work force which has nothing to do. This work force inherited an economic/business system and world built around and given birth to by a machine which does nothing but shuffle "facts," and these "facts" give rise to an enterprise system infinitely expandable. And so more lost ones were subsumed in the burgeoning whole.

Whatever you choose or are called to do, apart from doing that which you may know in your heart to be wrong, and I wouldn't advise you to do that, I think that you and I *are* all those freaks, or *are* those lilies of the field, and it is not given us to know the time in which we live. We may think we are creating masterpieces (and, in fact, we may be) or we may think we are bent over our tatting frames like Victorian women doing our "work." In any case, we are this: A part of the surplus shriven by Mother Earth.

The Bible says God loves us all.

THE DECORATION
OF JEWISH
HOUSES

My parents were the children of Ashkenazi immigrants. In my childhood home, and in the homes of my friends of like extraction, there was a feeling of tenuousness which expressed itself in the physical trappings. None of the homemakers knew quite what a home was supposed to look like. They had no tradition of decor, the adoption of which would be anything other than arbitrary.

When our grandparents left the *shtetl*, they brought nothing with them. What, in fact, could they have brought? There was, in their villages, no "Jewish" style of decoration, or furniture; there was no ornament, the look of what domestic artifacts there were was dictated by poverty.

There was no art in the Ashkenazi homes. And, as Jews,

there were no religious trappings beyond, perhaps, a *Kaddish* cup or a menorah.

What did our immigrant grandparents bring with them? Perhaps a photograph or two, perhaps a samovar; in short, nothing. And the children of those immigrants, my parents' generation, were raised in the New World in varying degrees, again, of poverty.

Surplus income was devoted to education of the young, to help them Get Ahead. As get ahead they did. They rose to prominence, in the Jewish way, in the professions which, since the days of Egypt, had been intermittently open to them: medicine, law, negotiation, commerce, banking, entertainment.

My parents' generation was in the rabid pursuit, first, of education, and then, of success, greatly assimilationist. They were, in my experience, largely Reform; and thought themselves "racially" but not "religiously" Jewish. They held to the increasingly sparse practice of religious ritual with a sense, quite frankly, of foolishness, as if to say, "I don't know why I'm doing this, and I share your ('you' being the world-at-large, which is to say, the Christian world) quite correct vision that all of this nonsense is *vastly* beside the point, and only serves to accentuate the differences between us, when we should, rightly, be concentrating on our similarities."

What did it mean, then, to be "racially" Jewish? It meant that, among ourselves, we shared the wonderful, the warm, and the comforting codes, language, jokes, and attitudes which make up the consolations of strangers in a strange land. We shared, among ourselves, Jewish humor, a pride in each other's accomplishments, a sense of sometimes intellectual and sometimes moral superiority to the populace-at-large. For were we not, as a group, socially conscious, socially committed, socially active, and dedicated to equal rights and consideration for all races and nations? Yes. We were. For all races except our inferior own.

In Mel Brooks's film *The History of the World, Part I,* Cloris Leachman, as Mme. Defarge, harangues the canaille in a wonderfully dreadful French accent. She says, "We have no home, we have no bread, we don't even have a *language*—all we have is ziz lousy *accent.*"

Similarly, our second generation had no language. Our parents eschewed Yiddish as the slave language of poverty, and Hebrew as the dead language of meaningless ritual. Yes, it was being spoken in Israel, and one could make Aliyah and *go* there, but, as the old joke has it, "what kind of job is that for a nice Jewish boy?"

For my generation, Jewish culture consisted of Jewish food and Jewish jokes, neither of which, probably, were very good for us.

We did not and we *do* not believe in the—let alone *ex-cellence*—*existence* of anything which could even remotely be referred to as a "Jewish Culture." We American Jews have been, and remain, quite willing to have the populace-at-large consider us second-class citizens—second-class citizens to be, in many ways, envied and scorned rather than oppressed and scorned, but nonetheless . . .

We Jews consider it a matter of course, for example, that there has never even been a Jewish candidate for *Vice* President.

In our lack of self-esteem, we, as a race, are happy and

proud that our country has progressed to the point that we can see a serious presidential candidate in Jesse Jackson. And this in *spite* of Mr. Jackson's rather blatant anti-Semitism.

His career awakens deep feelings of happiness that social justice is being done, and feelings of relief that the terrible racism in which we all grew up is beginning to wane. But we listen to his anti-Semitic remarks, we watch his endorsement of anti-Semitic leaders, we listen to his insulting disclaimers, and we think, "All right—to preserve the *peace*, we will all pretend that you don't mean it," and, singularly, in this aspect of our social life, we behave like fools.

Why then, my fellow Jews, have we never supported, or thought to support, why are we incapable of *envisioning* a serious presidential attempt by a Jew? Why does this prospect seem to us irrelevant and faintly ridiculous? As it seems to us faintly ridiculous that we might want in our cities major thoroughfares called Birnbaum or Schwartz?

We Jews know, even at the remove of Seventy Years—the span since my grandparents arrived in New York from the Pale till now—we know the warmth of camaraderie-in-exile, we know the warmth of self-deprecation. We know the warmth of the feeling of secret superiority, and of personal success against odds. But of the demand, of even the feeling of *rectitude* of the demand for absolute social equality, we know nothing very much at all.

We know that Black is Beautiful. We saw the young Jewish women of my generation *flock* to Black Studies programs at our universities, and we said, "Yes, they are drawn, quite rightly, in the strength of a correct and revolutionary cause. God bless them"; and we supported them in their support of

Black self-love at the same time we supported them in surgically re-carving their faces so that they would look less "Jewish."

We could not, as American Jews, feel that Jewish is Beautiful, that the sexy, vital, essential assertion of a just demand was within our power, *just* as it was and is within the power of the American Indians, or the Eskimos, or the American blacks. And *never* have we American Jews thought, let alone asserted, "Yes, *I* am beautiful. I come from a beautiful race." And we would say, with the irony which has been our most prized and useful possession for quite a few millennia: "I'm not going to say *that*—too *arrogant* . . . ," i.e., "too Jewish."

In our support of the moral, social, and emotional rights of the oppressed, we put ourselves, the Jews, behind not only every other racial group, we put ourselves behind the seals and the *whales*. Now, funny as that is, you, gentle reader, you tell me I'm wrong.

In what do we take pride? What symbols and what models do we possess?

We can point to the odd Jewish athlete with pride. What about Jewish business leaders, professional men and women? Entertainers? They are not sources of racial pride. Why not? Because they're simply doing what is expected of them. It is expected that we and our fellows will strive and succeed in the traditional pursuits of a landless people; in the pursuits of the mind.

But a Jewish *football* player . . . that person would stand as a magnificent and welcome freak. That person is an image which gets the heart beating a bit faster with pride. As does the success of the crypto-Jew.

"You know who's Jewish . . ." was a recurring phrase at my house, and in the homes of my contemporaries. That a Jew could rise to prominence, *particularly* in the entertainment industry, *without* being overtly Jewish, without playing Jewish parts, without being stereotyped, this filled us with a secret joy. Why? Because this person *had escaped*. This person had fulfilled a wild personal fantasy, they had "passed" with no effort, and, so, with no guilt, into the greater world from the lesser. (By the way, I wonder why it has escaped general comment that when the part of an *incontrovertible* "Jew" must be filled in the movies, it is *inevitably* filled by a non-Jew. Why? Because the Jew would look and act "too Jewish.")

Concomitantly, someone who obviously *was* Jewish and who sought to deny it, primarily through the adoption of a Christian religion, was, in our homes, an object of wonder and scorn. This person was despised as a weakling, and we thought (1) *I* can take it, why can't *you?*; and (2) How can you be so ultimately foolish as to trade your *Jewishness* for a greater acceptance in a community of strangers which (3) you aren't going to get anyway.

Or, to distill: What would induce you to renounce the only people who love you?

Because we do love each other very much. It is, I think, notable that we have *not* noted that we tend not to love ourselves.

We have our rare ballplayers, we have our tales of Charlie Chaplin and Cary Grant, we have the menorah or we had the samovar before Dad turned it into a lamp, we have our Jewish food (disappearing with the generation of the grandmothers), and we have our self-deprecating humor. (Yes, I know that it's funny. It is the funniest humor in the world, it's how I have made my living all my life, and, it *is* self-deprecating.)

But in our homes, in that which speaks of rest, of identity, we have no symbols. We do not know how a Jewish home (finally, we do not know how a *Jew*) is supposed to look.

We see in our homes the occasional and vaguely Semitic "quote," a Hebraised motto in English, a mosaic coffee table, a souvenir of a trip to Israel; or, in advanced cases, the display of a piece of Judaica. And that's a Jewish home to this day. The home of an outsider. We fit out our living places as if we were Yankees, we cast Laurence Olivier and Klaus Kinski as prototypical Jews. We have never known any better.

God bless those in all generations who have embraced their Jewishness. We are a beautiful people and a good people, and a magnificent and ancient history of thought and action lives in our literature *and lives in our blood*; and I am reminded of Marcus Garvey's rhetoric, in addressing the black populace: "Up you Mighty Race, you Race of Kings, rise to your feet, you can accomplish what you will."

We would say, "I already knew that," as we always have. Accomplishment has not been the problem, pride and enjoyment has.

When we let an anti-Semitic remark pass, with the silent thought, "What a sorry and misguided person"; when we shrug in sorrow at Jesse Jackson; when we sigh at the cocktail party when a "friend" says, "If you have been persecuted all these thousands of years, isn't it possible that you are doing something to bring it about?"; when we espouse, support,

and champion *every social cause* but our own, we contribute
to anti-Semitism.

I am sick of the Passover Seders at which we invite our
non-Jewish friends to engage in social colloquy, and which
inevitably degenerates into fair-minded discussions of how
authentic it is to be a Jew, how *authentic* is the state of Israel
and who is to blame for historical Jewish suffering. Are we
so poor that we can't even celebrate our own holidays, without
using them as a social *offering* to the larger group? Because,
finally, the social activism, the vast support of Liberal causes,
the invitation of our non-Jewish friends to the Seder, I'm
sorry, but finally, as much "good" as it may do, it stinks of
"take this but don't hit me."

I don't know what a Jewish home looks like.

I have never been to Israel. I wish my brothers and sisters
in Israel well, as do we all. It would be fine if we could end
our exile in this country, too.

A PLAIN
BROWN
WRAPPER

The periodic arrival of the Charles Atlas material disturbed me greatly. I was nine or ten years old, and had answered their ad in a comic book. The ad assured me that there would be no charge for information regarding the system of Dynamic Tension—the system which could and would transform the weakling into the well-proportioned strong man of the ads; the ad further assured me that the material would arrive in a plain brown wrapper.

The material did come, as advertised, in the plain wrapper. But it did not make me strong. It terrified me, because each free installment dealt with one thing and one thing only: my obligation to the Charles Atlas Company, and my progressively intransigent, incomprehensible, and criminal refusal to pay for materials received.

I dreaded the arrival of those envelopes; and when they arrived I slunk in shame and despair. I loathed myself for ever having gotten involved in this mess.

Was the whole Charles Atlas promotion geared to idiots and children? Looking back, I think it must have been. The Method of Dynamic Tension promised fairly instant strength and beauty at no cost to the consumer. And the vicious and continuous dunning letters played masterfully on the undeveloped ego of that idiot or child. I, one such child, thought, on receiving their threats: "Of course they are disappointed in me. I am weak and ugly. How dare I have presumed to take these fine, strong people's course? How dare someone as worthless as I have aspired to possess the secrets of strength and beauty? The Charles Atlas people have, as they must, recognized my laughable unworthiness, and my only defense against them is prayer."

For they were, of course, God—they offered me transformation in exchange for an act of sacrifice and belief. But I was unprepared to make that act.

The other religious experience of my youth was equally inconclusive and unfortunate. It was Reform Judaism: and though the God Jehovah, the God of Wrath and Strength and Righteousness spoke through the mouth of Charles Atlas, he was deemed quite out of place at the Sinai Temple.

The Rabbis were addressed by the title "doctor," the trumpet was blown in deference to the shofar, the ancient Hebrew chants and songs were rendered in Victorian settings, we went to Sunday School, rather than *shul*. There is nothing particularly wrong with these traducements of tradition, except this: they were all performed in an atmosphere of shame.

Untutored in any religion whatever, we youngsters were exposed to the idea of worshipper-as-revisionist. Our practices were not in-aid-of, but in-reaction-to. The constant lesson of our Sunday School was that we must be better, more rational, more up-to-date, finally, more *American* than that thing which had come before. And that thing which had come before was *Judaism*.

Judaism, at my temple in the 1950s, was seen as American Good Citizenship (of which creed we could be proud), with some Unfortunate Asiatic Overtones, which we were not going to be so craven as to *deny*. No, we were going to steadfastly bear up under the burden of our taint—our Jewishness. We were such good citizens that *although it was not our fault* that our parents and grandparents were the dread Ashkenazi, the "superstitious scum of Eastern Europe," we would not publicly sever our connection with them. We Reform Jews would be so stalwart, so American, so non-Jewish, in fact, as to Play the Game. We would go by the name of Jews, although every other aspect of our religious life was Unitarian. Our religion was nothing other than a corporate creed and our corporate creed was an evasion. It was this: We are Jews, and we are Proud to be Jews. We will express our Jewishness by behaving in every way possible exactly like our Christian Brethren, because what they have is better than what we have.

I found the Reform Judaism of my childhood nothing other than a desire to "pass"; to slip unnoticed into the non-Jewish community, to do nothing which would attract the notice, and, so, the wrath of mainstream America.

Why would America's notice necessarily beget its wrath? Easy: We were Jews, and worthless. We were everything bad that was said against us, we didn't even have a religion anymore, we'd given it up to placate the non-Jewish community, to escape its wrath.

What of the Wrath of Jehovah? He, too, was better left behind if we were to cease being Jews.

What was it, then, to be Jewish? Heaven forfend that it was to be part of a race, and spare us the wretched image of dark skins, loud voices, hook noses, and hairy hands.

Was it to be part of a religion? Of what did that religion consist? Every aspect of its observance had been traduced. Which of us Reform (which meant and means, of course, *reformed*, which is to say changed for the better, and, implicitly, penitent) Jews could remember the names, let alone the meanings, of those joyless holidays we attempted to celebrate? Those occasions—sabbath, holidays, bar mitzvahs— were celebrated with sick fear and shame. Not shame that we had forsaken our heritage, but shame that we had not forsaken it sufficiently.

One could both despise and envy Kissinger, Goldwater, and others who, though they had rejected the faith of their fathers, at least had the courage of their convictions.

The lesson of my Reform Temple was that metaphysics is just superstition—that there is no God. And every Sunday we celebrated our escape from Judaism. We celebrated our autonomy, our separateness from God and from our forefathers, and so, of course, we were afraid.

My coreligionists and I, eventually, sought out the God we had been denied. We sought God in Scientology, Jews for Jesus, Eastern Studies, consciousness-raising groups—all attempts to explain the relationship between the one and the all—between our powerlessness and the strength of the Universe. We sought God through methods not unlike Dynamic Tension—in which the powerless weakling, having been instructed in the Mysteries, overcame the Bully (the Juggernaut, the World) and so restored order to the Universe.

Here is my question: What was so shameful about wanting a better physique?

Why did such information have to come in a plain brown wrapper?

Why did the Charles Atlas Company know that such an endeavor needs to be hidden?

The answer is that the desire for a better physique was not shameful, but that we, the *applicants*, were shameful, and that we were intrinsically unworthy, the idea of weaklings such as ourselves desiring strength and beauty was so laughable that, of *course* we would want our desires to be kept secret.

That was why the dunning letters worked. They threatened to expose not that we had not paid our bills, but that we had the audacity to want a beautiful life.

And that was also my experience, as a child, of Reform Judaism. It was religion in a plain brown wrapper, a religion the selling point of which was that it would not embarrass us.

Thirty years later, I am very angry at the Charles Atlas Company, and at the Sinai Temple. Neither one delivered what they could and should have; more important, they had no right to instill in a child a sense of shame.

Thirty years later I am not completely happy with my physique, I am very proud of being a Jew, and I have a growing sense of the reality of God. I say to that no doubt long-demised Charles Atlas Company, You should be ashamed; and to the leaders of that Reformed Temple, What were you ashamed of?

WOMEN

A fellow called and asked me to write an article about women. My wife asked me what the call was about. I said they want me to write about women, but I don't *know* anything about women. "I know," said my wife. So I am writing this on a dare.

The first thing I realized about women is "they are people too." This came to me in my teen-age years, all of which were spent, in the vernacular, trying to get a leg over, and not having a *clue*. I was raised on James Bond and Hugh Hefner's Playboy Philosophy. Bond went through life impressing people with his gun, and Hefner went through life in a bathrobe; and the capper was that, of the two of them, Hefner was the one who actually existed.

"What were women?" I asked myself, and, one day the answer came, "They are people too." "Well, then," I thought, "they must have thoughts and feelings too!," and I have spent the last twenty-five years trying to figure out what those thoughts and feelings *are*.

The difficulty, of course, is one *wants* something from women: notice, sex, solace, compassion, forgiveness; and that many times one wants it sufficiently desperately that it clouds one's perception of what *they* want. And, in negotiations, it is never a good idea to lose sight of what your opponent wants.

Are all exchanges with women negotiations? Yes. If this seems like an inappropriate response, it is just that I do not know a stronger one than "yes."

Women, it seems to me, like to know who's in charge. And if it's not going to be them, they would like it to be you. The problem is that "in charge," in this instance, may be defined as "leading the two of you towards that goal which they have elected is correct." I will, at this point, compare dealing with women to dealing with children or animals. This is not to suggest that women are, in any way, inferior, but merely that children and animals are smarter then men.

Men have a lot to learn from women. Men are the puppydogs of the universe. Men will waste their time in pursuit of the utterly useless simply because their peers are all doing it. Women will not. They are legitimately goal-oriented, and their goals, for the most part, are simple: love, security, money, prestige. These are good, direct, meaningful goals, especially as opposed to the more male objectives of glory, acceptance, and being well-liked. Women don't give a tinker's damn about being well-liked, which means they don't know how to compromise. They will occasionally surrender to someone they love, they will fight until they have won, they will avoid a confrontation they cannot win, but they won't compromise.

Compromise is a male idea, and goes back to "being well-liked." Compromise means, "We're going to be meeting again in the future on some other issue, so don't you think it would be a good idea if *both* parties took something valuable away from this negotiation?" The female response is "no."

Which means women are not much fun to do business with.

George Lorimer, editor of the *Saturday Evening Post*, wrote, in 1903, that one should not do business with a woman; if they're losing, they'll add their sex to it; and if they're winning, they'll subtract their sex from it, and treat you harder than any man.

Well in *my* business, which is the Theater and Movies, I've found that's absolutely true. The coldest, cruelest, most arrogant behavior I have ever seen in my professional life has been—and *consistently* been—on the part of women producers in the movies and the theater. I have seen women do things that the worst man would never entertain the thought of—I do not imply that he would be stopped by conscience, but he *would* be stopped by the fear of censure, which takes us back to the inability to compromise.

The woman says, "I'm going to win *this* battle, and I'll worry about the *next* battle at that time."

Women have a tough time of it. Our society has fallen apart and *nobody* knows what he or she should be doing. A man usually deals with this by referring to his superiors, but he doesn't have to consider childbirth.

Is having kids an option, a necessity, a divine commandment? This has to be one of the most difficult questions in life, and it is one that half the population doesn't have to address, let alone answer.

Women, it seems to me, spend most of their childbearing years feeling guilty. When they're pursuing their career they feel, probably correctly, that they're short-changing their kids, or their own possibility of having kids. When they're having or raising kids, they feel the sands of their career-advancement clock running out on them. This is a bind I wouldn't like to be in; for a career and a home are very strong drives and desires. Popular publications inform the Modern Woman that she can have both to a completely full extent; but I never met a woman who believed it.

Women *want* to believe it, but my sad report is that they cannot, and so the working woman always has a segment of the popular thought to reproach herself with, *whatever* she chooses.

This dilemma deserves male sympathy. Males cannot, however, let themselves feel sympathetic, because we are somewhat guilty about how happy we are that we don't have the problem.

Men *generally* expect more of women than we do of ourselves. We feel, based on constant evidence, that women are better, stronger, more truthful, than men. You can call this sexism, or reverse sexism, or whatever you wish, but it is my experience.

The Governor of my State, a woman, refused to send the

National Guard to South America—an act of real courage and conviction. I expected it of her.

And I think men are reassured generally by the presence of women in previously all-male positions.

I feel about the woman governor, or airline pilot, or doctor, that she's less apt to be distracted than a man; I'm thankful for it. Are there *bad* women? Yes. I've already enumerated the single instance of women "producers." I know there are women criminals, I worked for a while in a women's prison. The inmates did a lot of crying, which seemed to me the appropriate response to the situation; and women, it seems to me, generally are more aware of what's going on than men are.

Over the years, I have come to rely completely on my wife's judgment of character; and am coming to rely on my daughter's ability to assess a situation correctly. The other day she got a splinter in her foot, and I got a tweezer and came over and stood in front of her, and she started to cry piteously. "*Why* are you crying?" I said. "I haven't even *touched* you yet . . ." "You're standing on my foot," she said.

Can we broaden this conceit of women having splinters in their feet, and men, their supposed saviors, adding to the discomfort? Women are, as we know, very much second-class citizens in this country.

As with any oppressed group, gains are not *awarded*, but won, and so the sight of the female airline pilot is, I think, a salutary reproach to the male; i.e., "I got here without you, and you can't begin to believe how hard it was. Do you think *you* could do as well?"

And to the young men in the audience who have not had

the benefit of the armed James Bond or the robed Hugh Hefner, I offer the following observations.

Our Western World is devolving into a more primitive, more effective society. When that more primitive society has taken root, you or your descendants will know how to get on well with women by obeying tradition, religion, and listening to your uncle. In the meantime: (1) be direct; (2) remember that, being smarter than men, women respond to courtesy and kindness; (3) if you want to know what kind of a wife someone will make, observe her around her father and mother; (4) as to who gets out of the elevator first, I just can't help you.

THE CENTRAL
PARK WOLF

Bicycles and dogs are not welcome on the upper track of the Central Park Reservoir. There are signs to the effect that they are not allowed, but the only sanction taken against offenders is a scowl from the passing runners to whose use the track is consecrated.

The custom of the track, for some reason, is for runners to proceed in a counterclockwise direction. At any given time the majority of runners may, in fact, be running clockwise, but they will be understood by themselves and by those they meet to be running *the wrong way*.

Prior to last Wednesday (March 28) the most provocative thing that ever happened to me while running around the reservoir was that a fellow sitting by the south pumphouse one day last spring pointed at me and for no conceivable reason, shouted "Boola Boola" each time I ran past him. I later realized I had been wearing my cousin's Yale sweatshirt at the time.

Last Wednesday morning I was jogging counterclockwise around the track and, walking slowly towards me, there was a German shepherd dog. I wished to exercise my perquisites and looked behind him for his owner to scowl at, but there was no one there.

The dog was white and wheat-colored, bruised along his left flank, and wore no collar.

"Wouldn't it be funny," I thought, "if the dog were mad. Then I would have to jump up on the fence. Somebody should call the police."

On my next lap, passing the south pumphouse and proceeding north up the Fifth Avenue side, I saw the dog again, still continuing in the same direction. A moment later various martial vehicles appeared in the bridle path below the running track.

The first were two police cars moving very quickly in reverse. They were followed by a squadroll—moving in the usual fashion, a white van, and more police cars.

I did not grow up in New York and so take great pride in understanding its quiddities. I was glad to grasp the nature of the procession at once: someone was filming a car chase. (Actually not an uncommon occurrence in and around Central Park.)

I started jogging north again when I heard the public address of one of the police cars blaring, "Get away from the dog. Get away from the dog." I looked back to see the cars had stopped even with the dog and the policemen were getting out of their cars.

"Great," I thought, "you are a rotten New Yorker. The dog is obviously the star of the sequence. He was *obviously* the object of the car chase. This must be a movie about some mad dog, or an escaped dog that knows the location of some jewels or something."

Thinking back I could see that the dog *must* have been trained to be able to proceed so regularly around the reservoir without human control. It was a trained dog and there must have been hidden cameras filming its progress around the reservoir, I thought. Perhaps I would be in the movie.

The Police kept screaming, "Get Away from the Dog. Get off the Reservoir. Get off the Reservoir." I looked back to see them climbing up the bank towards the dog, along with a man and a woman carrying nooses, who had just alighted from a white sedan blazoned A.S.P.C.A.

Jogging in place at the 86th Street stairs I asked a fellow runner if she knew what was going on. "It's a wolf," she said.

The wolf was frightened and took off clockwise around the reservoir. The Police and the A.S.P.C.A. ran back to their vehicles and gave chase.

I continued jogging north and had a good view of the chase—the Mars lights flashing, the amplifiers blaring, "Get away from the dog," startled runners scowling.

The chase ended at the north pumphouse with the Police and the A.S.P.C.A. officials clustered up on the concrete apron and the passers-by and joggers relegated to the lower bridle path.

Car and van radios were humming and people on the scene

were assuring others elsewhere that everything was all right.

Two very competent-looking A.S.P.C.A. Emergency Squad officers were sitting in their van. I went over to them and asked them what was going on. They told me they had caught a wolf. I asked them what was the wolf doing in Central Park. They told me it escaped from their East Side animal shelter the night before. They had been looking for it for several hours.

I asked them what was a wolf doing at their Manhattan shelter and they said its owner had brought it there.

When I told the story later to friends the most-often-held opinion was that the wolf had been bought small as a cute pet to commemorate some holiday or occasion and, like a turtle or an iguana or a baby alligator, or like a baby chick purchased for Easter, it had grown into its own and was no longer desirable as a pet.

INTRODUCTION

FROM

A PRACTICAL

HANDBOOK FOR

THE ACTOR

Most acting training is based on shame and guilt. If you have studied acting, you have been asked to do exercises you didn't understand, and when you did them, as your teacher adjudged, badly, you submitted guiltily to the criticism. You have also been asked to do exercises you *did* understand, but whose application to the craft of acting escaped you, and you were ashamed to ask that their usefulness be explained.

As you did these exercises it seemed that everyone around you understood their purpose but you—so, guiltily, you learned to pretend. You learned to pretend to "smell the coffee" when doing sensory exercises. You learned to pretend that the "mirror exercise" was demanding, and that doing it well would somehow make you more attuned on stage. You learned to pretend to "hear the music with your toes," and to "use the space."

As you went from one class to the next and from one teacher to the next, two things happened: being human, your need to believe asserted itself. You were loath to believe your teachers were frauds, so you began to believe that you *yourself* were a fraud. This contempt for yourself became contempt for all those who did not share the particular bent of your school of training.

While keeping up an outward show of perpetual study, you began to believe that no actual, practicable technique of acting existed, and this was the only possible belief supported by the evidence.

Now how do I know these things about you? I know them because I suffered them myself. I suffered them as a longtime student of acting, and as an actor. I suffer them second hand as a teacher of acting, as a director, and as a playwright.

I know that you are dedicated and eager—eager to learn, eager to *believe*, eager to find a way to bring that art that you feel in yourself to the stage. You are legitimately willing to sacrifice, and you think that the sacrifice required of you is subjugation to the will of a teacher. But a more exacting sacrifice is required: You must follow the dictates of your common sense.

It would be fine if there were many great master teachers of acting, but there are not. Most acting teachers, unfortunately, are frauds, and they rely on your complicity to survive. This not only deprives you of positive training but stifles your greatest gift as an artist: your sense of truth. It is this sense of truth, a simplicity, and feelings of wonder and reverence—

all of which you possess—that will revitalize the Theater.

How do you translate them onto the Stage? The answer to this question is reducible to a simple stoic philosophy: Be what you wish to seem.

Stanislavsky once wrote that you should "play well or badly, but play truly." It is not up to you whether your performance will be brilliant—all that is under your control is your intention. It is not under your control whether your career will be brilliant—all that is under your control is your intention.

If you intend to manipulate, to show, to impress, you may experience mild suffering and pleasant triumphs. If you intend to follow the truth you feel in yourself—to follow your common sense, and force your will to serve you in the quest for discipline and simplicity—you will subject yourself to profound despair, loneliness, and constant self-doubt. And if you persevere, the Theater, which you are learning to serve, will grace you, now and then, with the greatest exhilaration it is possible to know.

CONVENTIONAL WARFARE

SAHARA HOTEL,

LAS VEGAS POOLSIDE

 By seven P.M. the pool area was filled with conventioneers dressed in camouflage fatigues. It was announced that unsavory elements had taken hostages and were holed up on the third floor of the hotel. These elements, terrorists brandishing automatic weapons, appeared on the balcony and showed us the bound hostages.

Three men in black jump suits began rappelling rapidly from the hotel roof.

The cocky terrorists shouted their demands while the three men in black descended their ropes and took positions above and to the side of their balcony. A concussion grenade was lobbed into the terrorists' midst, the attacking forces swung onto the balcony, and the sound of simulated small-arms fire was heard. A woman in a violet ball gown appeared on the balcony beneath, and looked about wonderingly.

The black-suited S.W.A.T. team emerged from the smoke on their floor and held their weapons high, indicating victory was theirs. The conventioneers by the pool cheered—myself included. The woman on the second floor shrugged and went back into the building. Captain Dale Dye, U.S.M.C. (Ret.), then announced that the pugil-stick contest would begin.

This interested me particularly, as I had entered my name in the lists and was a contestant in said contest.

I waited for him to call my name and wondered whether I had the capacity to stand and slug it out with men, or whether I was just another wussy Eastern Intellectual with a marvelous gift for dialogue.

What was I doing in Las Vegas? I had come to have fun, and to hang out with my friend Bagwell and his friends.

His friends were the people at *Soldier of Fortune* magazine. The magazine was running its fifth annual convention at the Sahara Hotel. Bagwell, who makes knives for a living, is the knife editor of the magazine.

Soldier of Fortune was started ten years ago by Colonel Robert K. Brown, a veteran of the Special Forces; and the concerns of the magazine are fairly well represented by the activities at the convention. These included a three-gun (rifle, pistol, shotgun) competition with a hefty $40,000 in prize money; Operation Headhunter, a military-oriented five-mile cross-country obstacle/orienteering/endurance race; a parachute jump; a firepower demonstration; an arms show; sundry lectures; a pugil-stick competition; and a banquet.

The conventioneers were men—and a few women—in-

terested in the history, theory, and practice of warfare—
especially of unconventional or guerrilla war. They were, in
the main, former and current members of the armed forces,
law enforcement officers, gun aficionados, and, I suppose,
a couple of people like me who were just trying to get out
of the house.

I had never been to a convention of any kind before, and
I was getting a kick out of wearing one of those name tags,
which looked kind of silly when those other guys are wearing
them but feel rather comforting when you've got one on
yourself.

I found the conventioneers lovely people. I didn't agree
with some of the ideas, but then I don't agree with a lot of
my *own* ideas and seem powerless to rid myself of them.

One idea at the convention I found quite attractive was
that of unabashed patriotism. The fellows seemed to love the
idea of America in much the same way that someone else
might love the idea of The Theater—that is, as a perfect
institution.

The conventioneers also seemed to love the idea of Having
Fun.

I was already having fun. The cab from the airport dropped
me at the Sahara and the cabdriver asked me if I wanted to
flip for the four-dollar fare. I said okay and reached for a
coin. "*Uh uh*," he said, "we'll use *my* coin." Well, okay, I
thought, everybody's got to eat and he flipped his coin, and
he lost.

"What a great beginning to a Weekend with the Boys," I
thought, and checked into the hotel and started looking for
Bagwell.

The next morning I found him at his table at the arms show. Bagwell had seventeen of his knives laid out for display. He makes the knives at an open forge out behind his house in east Texas, and when I arrived he was putting on a display with one of them. He had a twelve-inch bowie knife and was about to cut four wrapped one-inch free-hanging strands of hemp rope with one swipe. The onlookers muttered among themselves that it was impossible, but I had seen him do it many times before. I asked him if *I* could try it when he got done. He gave a look that seemed to say, "Get away, boy, you are queering the pitch."

He then suggested, for good measure, that a friend of his take me for a walk. The friend introduced himself as an Air Marshal, late of the R.A.F.; and so the Air Marshal and I started on a leisurely tour of the arms show. We chatted about the State of the World (both dubious) and gave much attention to the tables laden with Interesting Stuff.

There were displays of holsters, freeze-dried foods for camping, and other exotica.

The fellow with the booth next to Bagwell's was selling blowguns.

They were tubes around four feet long with a mouthpiece at one end. He had put up a saucer-sized target on a wall thirty feet away, and all day long he was putting darts into the blowgun, going *whoosht*, just like in the movies, and the darts would appear in the target.

I asked him how accurate the blowgun was, and he told me that with just a little practice I could consistently hit a dinner plate at a hundred feet. I asked him if this would not involve my giving up smoking, and he told me that, on the contrary, the blowgun seemed naturally to increase one's lung capacity; and that the biggest problem his customers reported was the necessity of moving up to the next-sized shirt.

I wanted to try the blowgun, and kittenishly hung around his booth and waited for him to offer me a shot; but (and I suppose for sanitary as much as for ballistic reasons) he never did.

Both the Air Marshal and myself were entranced by a new pistol at the Beretta table (the pistol was a Teflon-finished military version of their 92SB, "The Gun That Guards Connecticut").

The Air Marshal said he was covering the convention for another magazine, and we both thought it would be a good idea to misuse the powers of the press and suggest to the Beretta people that we, as disinterested and powerful representatives of large organs of Public Opinion, might like to actually fire this pistol out at the range.

The Beretta people, with great reserve and no visible display of ill humor whatever, said they would see what they could do.

On the other side of Bagwell's display was the booth of the Free-World Congress of Paratroopers.

This organization had, in 1983 and 1984, taken paratroopers from all over the Free World to Israel to train with and jump with the Israeli Army for ten days. The organization was represented by Mike Epstein, a homeboy from North Clark Street in Chicago. Mike had jumped that morning with a group from the Phantom Division, an independent parachutists' club. The Phantoms, Mike told me, were running a jump school that could prepare even complete neophytes to jump—after one day's instruction—from operating aircraft.

I allowed as how I might like to try that myself, and Mike told me that I was too late to sign up for the program being run during the convention, but that I might like to attend the next Israeli Congress (Spring 1985). I told him I would like nothing more, and would only have to check with my wife, or, should *she* agree, with someone else.

Friday afternoon I attended a seminar on "Light Machine Guns: History, Evolution, Employment."

The seminar was given by "Machine Gun Pete" Kokalis, small-arms editor of *Soldier of Fortune*. Pete displayed some ten types of machine guns, including the MG42, or "Hitler's Zipper," so named for its very high (1,200 rounds per minute) cyclic rate; the MAG (Mitrailleuse à Gaz); the famous Bren gun, which Pete proclaimed the finest magazine-fed light machine gun in the world; and the hated American M-60.

Pete excoriated the workmanship and design of the M-60 at great length—the bipod legs break and it has at least eight separate parts that can be put in backwards and, in his own words, "Believe me, gentlemen, if they can be put in backwards they *will* be put in backwards." (I have spent fifteen years in the professional theater and knew what he was talking about.) Pete discussed kinds of fire with respect to ground, kinds of fire with respect to the target, methods of disassembly, and so on. As a sucker for technical information, I'm a cheap date *anyway*, but he was a *particularly* fascinating and concise lecturer, and when he field-stripped the MAG in about eight seconds I cheered with the rest.

Pete then told us something that made my day; he announced that in dealing with the Bren machine gun the biggest cause of Failure to Feed (that is, failure of the gun to chamber a cartridge) is failing to load the magazine in such a way that the rim of the second cartridge comes *in front of* the rim of the previous cartridge. I have made my living all my adult life on my ability to retrieve bizarre and arcane information, and this was a gem if I had ever heard one. I cherish it still.

□———□

This is what I had done up till Friday evening, when, to get back to it, I found myself standing by the pool and waiting to be called to fight in the pugil-stick competition.

A pugil stick is about five feet long. The last foot on each end is covered with a padded sausagelike affair. The contestants wear football helmets and approach each other from opposite ends of a one-foot-wide beam. The beam is over the swimming pool.

So, Captain Dale Dye announced the Pugil-Stick Competition, and I waited for them to call my name, meanwhile trying to remember everything I knew about close personal combat.

Everything I knew about close personal combat amounted to this: (1) I once had a girlfriend who was studying aikido, and she told me that one should never look into an opponent's eyes, as one might "see one's childhood" and be tempted to show mercy; (2) I had heard that a bloodcurdling scream can have the physiological effect of momentarily shocking an opponent into inaction; (3) I had read in *The Book of Five Rings*, a compendium of advice to the Japanese sword fighter, that an effective tactic is to thrust viciously, retire for the briefest split second, and, while your opponent is enjoying his nanosecond of peace, fall on him like the Wrath of a Just God.

Thus armed, I stood at attention next to my opponent while we were given our helmets, sticks, and jockstraps.

My opponent, whose name was Kogan, or something like that, wore a bathing suit. I, knowing something about psychology, was dressed in the full suit of camouflage fatigues I had bought that morning at the show. "Yes," I was indicating, "you may have some intention of getting wet, but I do not, I'll see you in hell."

On the command we mounted opposite ends of the beam. On the first whistle we were to "make an appropriately aggressive sound" and go into a "ready" stance. On the second whistle we were to advance along the beam, and, in the words of Captain Dye, we were to take no prisoners, we were not to *become* a prisoner.

I did scream. I did advance, and I knocked the son of a bitch into the pool. Shocked by my own good fortune, and giddy at the roars of the crowd, I then let my pugil stick fall.

The crowd suggested this rendered my victory void, and I had to dive into the pool, retrieve my stick, and fight the battle over.

The second time through I beat him again, and in the best tradition of the Eastern Intellectual, immediately started feeling sorry for him.

I then had to stand around in my soaked fatigues and wait for the next round of the elimination.

While I waited I watched high-roller types making book

on the outcome of the contest. "Yes," I thought, "these folks would bet on anything, and wouldn't sue you when they lose. What a change from the World of Show Business."

As I so mused my name was called to fight my second round.

My new opponent was a *biiiiig*—not to say huge—blond athletic type. We mounted opposite ends of the beam, and I said to myself, "Dave, *you* are going to Clean this Sucker's *Clock*."

I stared at his midriff so as to avoid his childhood, and, on the command, I gave the most warlike yell imaginable. All of my rage at this guy for being bigger and more fit than I, I put into that yell. I screamed my head off.

And he *wilted*. Imagine my surprise. He actually lost his composure and stepped falteringly backward on the beam. Captain Dale Dye then suggested that we both start again.

So we started again, gave our screams, advanced, and that big blond guy knocked my butt into the swimming pool. I never saw the one that hit me.

Chastened and moistened, I went back to my room to change for dinner, trying to find in my memory the appropriate verse of Kipling that might render my defeat an experience from which I might profit philosophically.

"If," of course, came immediately to mind; and then "Let us admit it fairly, as a business people should/We have had no end of a lesson: it will do us no end of good."

I changed out of my wet fatigues and into my Eastern Journalist Drag: blue oxford shirt, black knit tie, cunningly unconstructed cream-colored sports coat, blue jeans, and

Bass Weejuns. "Yes," I was proclaiming, "as you see, I am a noncombatant."

I dined with Mr. Bagwell; the Air Marshal; Bob Gaddis, a custom-knife dealer from Solvang, California; and Bob's assistant, Chris.

We had a long and very enjoyable steak dinner. The Air Marshal talked about his experience with the Gurkha Regiments, Bill Bagwell and Bob discussed the campaigns of Genghis Khan, and I told the one about the Screenwriter and the Elf.

The next morning I went out to the Desert Sportsman's Rifle and Pistol Club, about twenty miles out of town, for a demonstration of firepower.

I found a great seat on top of the Blue Diamond Fire Truck.

John Satterwhite, representing Heckler & Koch firearms, gave a demonstration with the shotgun. He tossed a clay pigeon in the air and shot it. He tossed two; he tossed five at once and got them all. He shot behind his back, he shot over his head, he tossed three eggs into the air and shot them. The man next to me said that one of John's favorites was a Chef's Salad: egg, lettuce, carrot, and tomato; but for some reason that wasn't part of the repertoire today.

Pete Kokalis and his crew fired off the machine guns he had lectured on yesterday.

A blue and silver P-51 flew by and looked very much like America. We waited for John Donovan, explosives and demolition editor of S.O.F., who had promised to blow up part of the mountain, but his part of the demo was the victim of faulty wiring. There was a mortar demonstration, and then we were informed, "This is what a fire fight sounds like," and the machine guns and the mortar all fired at once and for an extended period; and I was very glad to have spent the sixties fighting the battle of Montpelier, Vermont.

As the demonstration ended, the Blue Diamond Fire Truck sped off to extinguish a small brush fire that the tracers had started on the mountain, and I hitched a ride back to town with the Beretta people.

They found a convenient hillside, and, very graciously, they let me try out their new pistol. I frightened the hell out of some tin cans at sixty or seventy yards, and then, content that those cans had been amply warned, we all rode back to Vegas.

That night the concluding banquet was held, John Donovan, emcee, took some good-natured ribbing over his inability to blow up the mountain. The Colors were beautifully presented by Fox Company, 2nd Battalion, 23rd Marines, Las Vegas. Various awards were given out, anticommunist speeches were made, and we all stood to sing "God Bless America."

Donovan closed the banquet with a toast: "Here's to Rape, Pillage, Plunder, and may 'Son of a Bitch' become a Household Word."

The next morning I took a cab to the airport. The cabbie asked how long I'd been in Vegas. I told him two days. He asked me how I liked it, and I told him I considered it my second home.

MEMORIAL DAY, CABOT, VERMONT

Today Vermont celebrates Memorial Day. The Country as a whole was "let out from school" on Monday, and the Post Office was closed; but Vermont celebrates today, one day later; and, locally, it was not just another amorphous holiday, but an occasion of remembrance.

Down at Harry's Hardware—the Rialto of Cabot—we were drinking our morning coffee. Doc Caffin bemoaned the fact that most of the younger Vets, that is, the Vietnam War Vets, couldn't take off work to attend the Ceremony.

Chunk Barrett is the ex-postmaster of Cabot. He told me that when he was a child there was something called the Ladies Relief Corps, an organization originally formed to honor Veterans of the War of Independence. On Decoration

Day, Chunk said, these ladies would lay a wreath at the cemetery and throw blossoms in the river off the Elm Street Bridge. "When I came home from the Navy," Chunk said, "that had all stopped for some reason. So I started it up again."

The Memorial Day Service is now under the direction of Bob Davis, who used to run the Creamery (that is, the Cabot Farmers Dairy Co-Operative).

Chunk and I were standing in front of his house when the Parade came by. Doc Caffin carried the National Colors, Bunchy Cookson, who owns the local garage, carried the flag of the American Legion. Bob Davis marched with an old M-1.

Also in the parade were an Air Force Major, four grade-school children bearing wreaths, and a troop of nine Brownies carrying lilac blossoms. They were followed by an element of the Cabot High School band.

The parade halted on the Village Green, which is right across from Chunk's house. They drew up opposite the Civil War Memorial Obelisk. The Cabot band played "My Country 'Tis of Thee." One of the high school students spoke on the history of the Memorial Day Observance. The Air Force Major spoke eloquently on the sacrifice made by the young men and women who, in every generation, have heeded the Call to Arms, and defended American Interests. Several of the Cabot students read poems about Flanders Fields.

Now, I thought, these young people do not know where Flanders is. They do not know that the fields were made red with blood. They do not know that, in Britain, "Play Up and Pay the Game" sentiment of the Flanders Fields poetry marked the end of an era, the end of the Martial Spirit in

Britain, and the end of an Empire. They do not know that a complete generation of British men died in the First World War. They can have no idea *why* those men died—and neither can you or I. Undoubtedly one hundred years from now the causes of World War II, that "just" war, will seem equally obscure to the schoolchildren. We think we know why our parents fought. They fought to defend themselves. They fought for their lives.

In my community and numbered among my friends are veterans of World War II, a veteran of the Luftwaffe, a member of the Dutch Resistance, and a Jewish war refugee driven out of Warsaw by the Nazi Terror. I was born in 1947, and these people are part of a historical past to me, much as the Veterans of Vietnam will be to the schoolchildren on the Cabot lawn.

All our conflicts fade into antiquity. The most furiously fought issues are reduced to captions in the history books: "They were bitter rivals."

In the most magnificently written speech of exhortation in the English language, Shakespeare writes, "Old men forget and all shall be forgot but this they shall remember with advantage," etc.

And who among us remembers St. Crispin's Day?

The schoolchildren know nothing of war. They are raised on the unfortunate destructive rhetoric of confrontation, just as I was thirty years ago. They are brought up to believe the world's divided into *we* and *they*; and *we* are always right. And *they* are always wrong.

The Cabot children also have a great gift: They are part of a community that loves them. And they're present at the

Memorial Day ceremony not to honor the slain of our various wars; but to honor their living elders who desire that the children come and participate in this ceremony. Weighted against the tradition of Our Gallant Dead, the children have in their midst the immediate example of their Fathers and Grandfathers, who do not talk about the War—those that I have met—except to wonder often what it was that we were fighting for.

Can it be that this Luftwaffe veteran, and this veteran of the Resistance were once sworn to kill each other? Can it be that our ally "Gallant Russia" is the devil incarnate and the world is only large enough for them or us? *Why* is it that, once again, the race is intent on self-destruction?

On the Village Green, there are four schoolchildren carrying wreaths. At the end of the ceremony, one wreath is laid at the Civil War Obelisk, and taps is played by two buglers from the High School. Bob Davis announces that the parade will re-form and proceed down to the Town Hall, then to the Bridge, and then to the Elm Street Cemetery. That accounts for the remaining wreaths, and I'm glad that, once again, flowers are being thrown on the river, as they were when Chunk Barnett was young.

There is something in these same families performing these same traditions in the same spot for over two hundred years. In this small town, the Fourth of July and Memorial Day are observed with speeches and songs. The community is not abashed by public display of those things which unite it. Life in a farm community seems to instruct the young to think what is right and then to do what is right.

In Cabot the Thirtieth of May is flanked by the Memorial

Day Parade and a demonstration against the Federal Government.

Tonight there is a meeting at the Blue Mountain High School in Wells River, Vermont. The U.S. Department of Energy is searching for a site to dump high-level nuclear waste, and one of the proposed sites is in Spruce Mountain National Forest, about ten miles from the town of Cabot, where I live.

Down on Main Street, Cabot, the question of the week is: "Are you going to the meeting?," and the question is rather rhetorical, because everyone is going to the meeting.

Blue Mountain High School originally scheduled the meeting in the home economics room. Aware of the mounting local interest, they rescheduled it for the auditorium. It has now been rescheduled for the gym, and speakers have been set up outside the gym to accommodate the overflow. Buses and carpools have been arranged to transport the citizenry. In the last two days, full-page ads have appeared in the local papers saying "tell (your representatives) that you will oppose the nuclear poisoning of Vermont with all the legal means at your disposal, *and that you expect them to do likewise.*" The ad goes on to quote General Ethan Allen in a letter to Congress, 1781: "I am as resolutely determined to defend the independence of Vermont as Congress is that of the United States."

I wrote the ads.

It is no longer a novel experience for me to see my words in print, or to hear them performed on stage or in the movies. But when I saw these ads in print I was shocked. "Surely," I thought, "a private citizen can't just walk into a newspaper and place an ad exhorting the populace to oppose the Federal Government." But such, it seems, is, in fact, the case.

The day is a celebration of two great American Imperatives: the Necessity of Community Action and the Necessity of Independent Thought. The poem "In Flanders Fields" ends: "If ye break faith with us who die,/We shall not sleep, though poppies grow/In Flanders fields." The Vietnam Vets are working in the Creamery, and they can't get off work to come to the Parade. This evening they will certainly be too tired to come to the Antinuclear Meeting. Most of the older folks will be there. The strong Vermont tradition of Town Meeting has, perhaps, ingrained in them the notion that, perhaps, they *are* the government. The "ringer" in the town is me, and I'm still amazed that the newspaper printed my ad. That such a thing is actually possible awes me.

Was this freedom worth fighting for?

Yes. It was and is worth fighting for; and if history is supposed to tell that the fighting and the freedom were not connected, those that *did* the fighting thought they were. And most of them, I am sure, went to those wars for the same reason we are going to the Antinuclear Meeting tonight: to secure the benefits of life, liberty, and the pursuit of happiness for ourselves and our posterity.

HARRY'S HARDWARE

In the back room of Harry's Hardware Store on Main Street, Cabot, Vermont, there is a framed illustration—salesman in a frock coat is speaking to a man in coveralls. The man in coveralls holds a brass-bound mahogany carpentry level in his hands. He is obviously a foreigner, of German or Scandinavian descent, and the illustration's artist has caught a mood of desire and apprehension as he looks down at the plane.

This carpenter is about to make a purchase on which his livelihood will depend. He is resolute and will not be swayed either by empty salesmanship or by his own desires. The salesman knows this. He knows the man will make up his own mind but, perhaps, he could use a bit of help. Perhaps

the carpenter is unacquainted with American brands, or perhaps he has overlooked the trademark.

The salesman is making his customer a promise—he is
binding his *own* reputation to that of his wares. He points to
the level. His words, printed on the bottom of the poster,
read: "That's made by the Stanley Rule and Level Company."

The illustration is a cardboard counter display from the
1920s. It hangs above a counter full of old American and
English molding planes. Around the room are tables full of
old chisels, drills, and rules; on the wall are displayed old
saws and levels like the one in the illustration.

Chris Kaldor bought the store from Harry Foster in 1982
and Harry moved up the hill.

In the front room Chris sells hardware, clothing, ammunition, fishing tackle, farm and building supplies, and
sundries.

He has hot coffee, and there is a table to imbibe at while
discussing the weather and other variables.

Last month the monotony of Vermont Mud Season was
broken by discussion of the Mystery Tool.

Chris bought a mixed lot of antique tools and found in it
an object of this description: a curly-maple handle six inches
long and flared at the lower end, a blacksmith-wrought head
four inches long and looking like a cross between a logging
hook and a miniature adze.

Chris wrapped a dollar bill around the handle with a rubber
band and left the tool up by the cash register. The first person
to identify it correctly would win the dollar.

The answer most often given was, "I don't know, but it

looks very familiar"; followed in frequency by, "I've *seen* one before, but I forgot what it is."

FOURTH OF JULY

The Cabot Parade draws visitors from all over New England. It is an "Old-Fashioned" Fourth of July, with floats, a band, a barbecue, and a midway.

At the midway you can throw baskets for a quarter in hope of winning a prize, you can throw baseballs at a target in the hope of dunking a town dignitary in a tub of water. Last year the dignitary was the school principal. Red Bean is usually on the midway with his collection of ancient and beautifully restored gas engines, and you look at those green and red masterpieces and feel a bit of what they must have meant to a farmer in 1890, a five-horse engine to drive a winch, or a conveyor belt, or a log splitter, or pull a tractor.

The Parade is usually scheduled to begin at eleven, and usually begins by twelve. It's organized by Eunice Bashaw, who drives the school bus; and Eunice rules on the acceptability of the entries—this acceptability based in the main on the application being in on time, and even this criterion is pretty elastic. I don't think she'd exclude a nice float driven by people of good will who just happened to show up at the last second. Eunice also appoints the Secret Judges and administers the Awarding of the Prizes (usually $100 for Best Float, $50 for Most Humorous, and $50 for Most Inventive). I am acquainted with these categories as I have had the honor, three times, to be one of the Secret Judges of the Parade, and am *still* smarting about some of the compromises I had to make.

The Parade is usually made up of an Honor Guard, several musical entries, home-grown statements like Ed Smith's "Summer in Cabot" float of 1985, which featured Ed and his family swathed in woolen overgarments and huddled around a potbellied stove; various fire engines from surrounding towns, The Bread and Puppet Theater, a truck from the Creamery, and so on.

The Parade forms below the bridge on Elm Street, and marches past the town's three businesses, the Post Office, and down Main Street to the recreation field and the chicken barbecue.

Down at the Hardware Store, the community is united in discussion of the unique calendar of northern Vermont: haying, deer season, January Thaw, Mud Season, and black flies; and the universal calendar of human endeavor, wives, mothers-in-law, and why nothing seems to be as well made as it used to be.

I have been coming up to Cabot for twenty-two years, I've been shown by the local people how to cut and chop wood, how to make a hunting knife at a forge, how to ride a horse. As an outsider and a transient, I have been the recipient of that same patience and courtesy the Stanley Salesman in the poster was showing to the foreigner in the poster—a generosity founded on deep self-respect and pride.

The Mystery Tool at Harry's was identified variously as a child's miniature adze, a small picaroon, and a garden implement of some sort.

The dollar prize was finally awarded to an elder citizen who identified the tool as a wood scribe, i.e., a device for incising a line on wood.

The consensus among Harry's patrons was that the tool was *not* a scribe, but that, barring incontrovertible identification, the older fellow should claim the buck, his guess being the most likely. The tool now hangs on the wall in Harry's back room.

THE LAUREL CROWN

Roy Jones, an American boxer, fought his way to a decisive victory over Park Si Hun, a South Korean, in the final round of the Olympics. He was then robbed of his gold medal by corrupt and partisan judges. Jones had outboxed, outfought, and outshone the other man in the ring.

American commentators described it as a walkover, and the South Korean radio, during the last round, remarked, quite rightly, that Park would need a knockout to win the gold, as he was hopelessly behind on points.

When the fight ended, Jones and his corner were proud and elated as they waited for the judges' pro forma announcement that he had won. It was then proclaimed that,

3-2, the judges had awarded the gold to Park. The referee's jaw dropped. Jones and his team were stunned, then shocked, then furious.

Jones had fought and trained for years. He had defeated his opponent, and then learned that venality, guile, and corruption are not respecters of place—that even in the most sacrosanct arena, his dedication, pain, struggle, and victory could be brazenly denied him without shame.

The highest Olympic award today is the gold medal. In the Olympic Games of antiquity, it was the laurel crown. That crown is rooted in mythology.

Apollo fell in love with the nymph Daphne and pursued her. She abhorred the thought of marriage and fled. He ran mercilessly after her. As it became clear that he would soon possess her, she prayed to her father, Peneios, to preserve her by changing that form that had so enthralled Apollo. Her prayer was answered. She was changed into a laurel tree.

The laurel crown, adorning victors in war and the Olympic Games, was understood to be an ironic reminder that victory is hollow—that most times, on achieving our goal, we find it has changed and is no longer that which we pursued— that, indeed, we ourselves have changed in the pursuit.

Many of us, I am sure, thought: "Reject the silver medal. Don't mount the podium and glorify this vicious farce." But Jones faced the camera and accepted the silver medal. His presence on the podium was an irrefutable indictment of his judges.

It was also a magnificent lesson—that his sportsmanship and excellence had carried him to triumph in the Games and would carry him to triumph beyond them, that the true meaning of victory is better found in the wilting laurel crown than in the seemingly incorruptible medal of gold.

The Olympics are ideally a celebration of the spirit. The Olympics have seen no greater example of it than Jones and his victory.

SOME LESSONS
FROM TELEVISION

BILL MACY'S ACTING CLASS,

LINCOLN CENTER, 1988

 I was watching the television show *Hill Street Blues* last night. A woman was playing the part of a transsexual; that is, a woman was playing the part of a woman who had once been a man. As I watched, I thought, "What a brilliant characterization." Which characterization, of course, consisted in her having the understanding and the self-control *to not do a thing.* She let the script do the work. We were told by the script that she had once been a man. And why should we disbelieve what we had been told? So we, the audience, accepted it, and the actress's correct understanding aided our enjoyment of the script. *She did not torture the audience to assuage her feeling of not having worked hard enough.*

How, by extension, would one characterize a King, a Policeman, a Doctor, a Thief? Well, by extension, one would characterize them in just the same way. By leaving the characterization in the hands of the writer, which is where it belongs, and the only place where it can be safely dealt with. Why? Because there *is* no meaning to the concept of "a king." *King* is not a character, it is a title; and, as the Bard reminds us in *Twelfth Night*: "*Cucullus non facit Monacum*," the Cowl does not make the Monk, the Title does not make the Man or Woman.

But surely, you say, there is such a thing as "regal bearing." Yes, surely there is, and it is possessed by many not in the Royal Line, and many kings do not possess it, and, in fact, the possession of Regal Bearing by a king is nothing other than coincidence.

You and I, that is to say, the audience, will accept anything we are not given a reason to disbelieve. This is the reason the actor must study vocal and physical technique. These techniques are studied solely to render the actor sufficiently uninflected to allow the audience to accept him in a multiplicity of roles.

What else can be learned from this woman on *Hill Street Blues*? This: We judge people by first impressions. We have all had the experience of liking a girl, or boy, from afar, and having a friend say, "Oh, he or she is a snob," or of a potential business partner, "He's a deadbeat," et cetera, and it is then well-nigh impossible to separate those labels from our feelings about the person in question *irrespective of how that person acts.*

How can the actor employ this phenomenon? Well, as I have said, by understanding that the audience will accept what The Script has told them is true, and that the actor need not touch it. Also, the actor can profit in this way: By *endowing* the other actors, those with whom he plays, with the essential characteristics of the scene.

I stress the *essential*, rather than the *superficial* characteristics of the scene. That is, it is not important that one's opposite player is A King, it may be important that it is *as if* he could give you a job. It may not be important that the script characterizes someone as A Lackey, but it may be important that it is *as if* he owed you a favor.

Our minds will accept these endowments, just as the audience does, if we state them simply. It will *not* accept these suggestions if we *perform* them, but it will accept them if we *act* on them. We don't have to *believe* them (no more does the audience), we simply have to act *as if*.

We have all had the experience of an *endowment* changing our perceptions of our fellows. For example, we are told that the boss is a much-decorated hero of combat; or that the underling is a brilliant pianist; or that the Nobody at the bar is an infallible success with women; or that the apprentice is worth five million dollars. We hear and we *act* on these endowments all the time. When we are told that the apprentice is vastly wealthy, we somehow can't quite see her the same way, *can* we?

This is the fun part of acting. This is "playing." It is the simple solution to a complex problem, the problem of "characterization." There is no such thing, for the actor, as characterization. Character, as Aristotle reminded us, is just habitual action. We know a man's or woman's character *by what they do*, and we tend to blatantly disregard what they say about themselves, particularly and especially when those things which they say about themselves are obviously designed to induce us to respond to them in some manner which will redound to their own self-interest. We are no fools. We know when someone is mouthing off in order to get in our pants, or in our pockets. We know that we will withhold judgment of someone's character until we see *how they act*. We know it when we meet them at a party, and we *also* know it when we meet them in the theater.

Characterization is taken care of by the author, and if the author knows what he is about, he *also* will avoid it like the plague, and show us *what the character does* rather than having the character's entrance greeted with "Well, well, if it isn't my ne'er-do-well half-brother, just returned from New Zealand."

Remember that the psychology of those in the audience is exactly the same as the psychology of those on the stage.

The simple magic of the theater rests in the nature of human perception—that we all want to hear stories. And the stories we like the best are those told the most simply.

This magic, if correctly understood, leads to happy actors and a happy audience. It is the gift given by God, and not the dull technical manipulations of some smarty-pants "artist" with a good idea. As Stanislavsky told us: Any director who feels he has to do something "interesting" with the text doesn't understand the text.

I was also watching *Cagney and Lacey*. Here we have Tyne Daly, surely one of our *finest* actresses, a model artist and a delight to watch in any part. In this episode, she, and her copolicewoman, played by Sharon Gless, go into a building which a sign identifies as a Meat-Packing Firm.

As Tyne goes into the place, she has been directed to sniff. Why? She was directed to sniff to *further* inform us that she was in a meat-packing firm. Well. We knew that already. We all saw the sign. And nobody needs to be told twice. It's like saying, "I love you. (*Pause*) And I mean it." If we believed "I love you," we certainly *don't* believe it when we get the addendum.

We saw the sign, we saw the hanging slabs of meat. We knew we were in a meat-packing firm. Why did the director feel compelled to help us along. To tell us how the place *smelled?* Why? How the placed smelled was not part of the play. How do I know? Because it wasn't part of the *action* of the play. Tyne was acting the part of a woman In Great Danger. Why would such a woman take time out *to comment* (which is what she was directed to do) on the smell of a place in which the overriding, the essential element was: *This is a place in which I might be killed.*

No. *Also:* We didn't wonder how the place smelled *until she sniffed.* And *when* she sniffed we *doubted* that she was in the place the sign told us she was in. Why? Because we sniff to identify a surprising and, usually, unpleasant odor. That is why we sniff. And Tyne was directed to do the opposite. *Not* to identify, but to *comment.* Here she is, involved in trying to Apprehend a Dangerous Killer, and we see her directed to take time out to comment that "her character" finds the smell of hanging beef unpleasant. And when she *did* that, not only did we doubt the *place,* but we doubted the *action*, even when performed by this magnificent artist.

Further, if the *place* of action is not germane to the plot (i.e., The Room in Which My Sister Secreted My Share of the Inheritance), *leave it out*, you writers. We're better off in a Dark Wood, a Light Wood, a Drawing Room. Why? Because then we'll watch the Action.

And Realism, in this day and age, is an attempt *to convince*, *not* an attempt *to express* (as it was in the time of Stanislavsky).

That is why "realistic" acting rings so false. "Realism"— the concern with minutiae as revelatory of the truth—was an invention of the nineteenth century, when The Material seemed to be, and, perhaps, was, the central aspect of life. Our own time has quite understandably sickened of The Material, and needs to deal with things of The Spirit.

So we must, simply, lay aside our boring and fruitless pursuit of the superficial and dedicate ourselves to Action, which is to say to *Will* as the expression, as it is, of the Spirit.

We do not need to characterize. We only need, simply as possible, to *elect* and to *do* what we elect to do.

Jimmy Stewart, in accepting an Academy Award, thanked all the directors who had, over the years, broken him of his "good intentions."

What does this mean? Actors who want to take charge of items *not in their job description* make themselves and the audience unhappy. (Just as the director's good intention to have Tyne Daly sniff, his desire to "help" the audience, hurt the scene.)

Actors who want to change the script, who want to correct the director, or to direct the other actors, or to criticize the audience, these people are working too hard, and to no purpose whatever. There is only so much psychic energy. Any energy devoted to one task will be subtracted from another.

Similarly, the audience only has so much energy. If they are watching the heroine navigate her Progress through a Dark Night of Danger, they are going to be paying very close attention. When we show these attentive people the heroine sniffing at the smell of meat, they are going to accept that clue as as important as the unexpected creak of a door, and they are going to be disappointed and confused when they realize that it is not a clue at all, it is merely a *comment*.

It is the strength to resist the extraneous that renders acting powerful and beautiful.

A
THANK-YOU
NOTE

I was recently riding on a London bus. Some one was smoking. The association of the rocking of the bus and the smell of good, nonfiltered cigarettes took me back twenty-five years.

In my mind, I was, again, riding various Chicago buses to various jobs, schools, or assignations. And as I rode those beautiful buses, which felt so much like home, I smoked my Luckies and I devoured the world's literature.

I loved those bus rides and I loved those books. I was surprised and, I suppose, charmed, to see that I still associate the rocking, the diesel smell, the toasted smell of someone else's cigarettes, with those vast, long novels—especially those of the Midwesterners: Dreiser, Sherwood Anderson, Willa Cather, Sinclair Lewis. Those big, long books about the prairies that never end, about an emptiness in the stomach, about a certain feeling, almost a love, of pain.

The old librarian at my high school once found me reading a paperback copy of *Lady Chatterley's Lover*, and chided me for my errant taste.

He felt he was expressing his regard for me by showing me his disappointment. He pursed his lips and said, "Why do you read that stuff?" and even at the time I felt sad for him, and rather pitied him both as a fool missing the pleasures of literature, and as a weakling incapable of constructing a better sexual advance. What effrontery. But he had seen a lot of me. I spent all of my after-school time in the man's library, reading anything that had not been assigned.

In high school class I did read the assigned *A Tale of Two Cities*, which, apart from *A Christmas Carol*, is the only thing of Dickens I have ever been able to abide.

Call me a philistine, but I prefer the boredom and repetition of Sinclair Lewis, and the painful sincerity of Dreiser, to butchers named "Mr. Cuttymeat," and so on; and I say, further, what of Thackeray, or even Wilkie Collins, either of whom Dickens, in my estimation, was not fit to fetch tea for. But then I seem to always get it wrong, as the Librarian said. I think that Dostoyevsky is not fit to be mentioned in the same breath with Tolstoy, nor Henry James with Edith Wharton. I do not like the tortured, and I prefer the truth in straightforward honesty to the "art" revealed by whatever it is that we call talent.

Well, there, I've said it. And as long as I'm *coming out*, I might as well add that I think that Mozart couldn't adjust Bach's shoe buckles—an opinion which can be of interest to *no* one, and which I include solely because I have been trying to work it into cocktail conversation for many years and I have recently stopped drinking.

And I stopped smoking cigarettes long enough ago that they, when smoked by someone else, smell awfully good to me. They take me back to the days of my youth, and the beginning of my Love of Literature.

I have great gratitude to George Eliot, to Willa Cather, to the men and women beyond genius, to the simple writers to whom the only meaning of "technique" was clarity. These people have been my great friends, my teachers, my advisers, for twenty-five years, from the time I thought Anna and Vronsky were romantic older people, to my last reading, when I was shocked to find that they were unfortunate young people.

To those writers—*how* can I feel they are dead—

Thank you for the insight that the only purpose of literature is to delight us. Thank you for your example. I am sorry that you were in pain. Thank you for your constancy.

STANISLAVSKY
AND THE
BEARER BONDS

Stanislavsky once asked his students to deter-mine how to act the following scene: An accountant brings home from his office a fortune in negotiable bearer bonds, which he must cata-logue. Living with him is his wife, their newborn child, and his wife's idiot brother.

He arrives home while his wife is bathing the baby. The idiot brother is seated by the fireplace staring into the fire.

The accountant wants to get started on his work before dinner so he sits down at the table, strips the wrappers off, which he throws in the fire, and starts cataloguing the bonds.

His wife calls from the next room, "Come and see how cute the baby is." The accountant gets up and goes into the next room. The idiot brother takes the bearer bonds and begins throwing them into the fire and laughing. The laughter draws the accountant back into the room. As he sees what is happening, he thrusts the brother out of the way, in an attempt to get the remaining bonds out of the fire before they burn. The brother hits his head on an andiron and dies. The wife comes running into the room and sees her brother dead. She then screams, "Oh my God, the baby!" and runs back into the other room, followed by her husband, where they both discover the baby drowned in the bath.

Stanislavsky told his students that when they know how to analyze and perform that scene, that *then* they would know how to act.

Any school of theatrical thought is short-lived. A "school" really only exists in retrospect; the title is a post-facto assessment of the naturally occurring similarities between the works of several artists, each affected secondarily by the work of the others and, more important, by the time in which they live.

During the period of the artist's healthy production, the work of the individual artist, and of the collective unconscious expressing itself through the artistic community, is the *most effective way* for the artist to express what he or she sees; and innovations in technique (which is what the audience perceives as *style*) arise *only* to allow the artist to express more simply and forcefully what he or she knows to be the *most realistic vision of the world.* Eventually the superficial—i.e., reducible and copyable—aspects of this new technique are adopted by those *without* a vision as the "correct" way, not, as in the case with the prime creator, to express a realistic vision of the world, but, now, "to create Art." And while the ecstatic was becoming, in the consciousness of the nonartists, the formulaic, the true artist was moving on to a new vision, driven not by the need to be different from the imitators, but by a more basic need to explore the unexplored.

So that any "school" of art is short-lived, and none can possess a final "say" as to the correct technique. Technique arose out of an unrepeatable moment in the life of the world, and in the life of that one part of it which was the individual artist.

We cannot say that any technique is more correct than another, cave painting is not more "real" or more "beautiful" than the perspectives of Caravaggio or the semi-abstract skies of Turner; all rely on conventions; and when we say that any work is an absolutely realistic depiction, we mean only that we find it beautiful—it responds to some of our *preconscious* views of the world; i.e., it reflects *what we think, but we didn't know we thought* until we saw the painting. In the words of Mr. Wilde, "We didn't have these pea soup fogs till someone described them."

Again, there is no "correct" school of any artistic thought. There is, however, a fairly good test of an *incorrect*, which is to say, a *useless*, school (a useless school of artistic thought being one that does not serve the purpose of communion between the artist and the audience on this subject: the true, hidden nature of the world).

We may assume that a school of artistic thought is useless when it is universally accepted as being the only and exclusive possessor of truth.

A new artistic vision, a new school of thought, a new satisfying artistic "reality" must coalesce around the rebel. It is not the job of the audience, not the job of the amateur, it is only the job of the true artist to, not "supersede," but *ignore* the obvious accepted standard of artistic excellence in favor of the vision which to him or her is real. The audience, the amateur, the critic—*their* job, in the face of this new vision of reality, is to *resist*, to the point where the determination of the artist overcomes their resistance. This is the scheme of aesthetic natural selection.

New artistic vision grows in absolute contravention of this accepted thought. This is its fertile soil. In Berlin, in the 1870s, Stanislavsky saw a traveling troupe of players whose performance was the opposite of the formalized presentational theater of the day. They were the protégés of the Duke of Saxe-Meiningen. This troupe treated each new play as a new problem in psychology; and rather than (in the accepted procedure) handing each actor only his or her lines, and assembling the cast several nights before the performance, said cast to act in support of the star around whom the performance was built, the Saxe-Meiningen troupe saw the play as an exercise in psychology. They analyzed the play in its entirety, and each individual part, to find the unifying theme, and then related that theme to congruent events in the life of the individual player, so that the actor trained to bring to the stage the message of the play, the actions of the character *as he believed it to relate to his own life.*

This was a revolutionary departure, and Stanislavsky, the son of a wealthy manufacturer, was sufficiently moved to forsake his class, adopt a foreign stage name (his family name was Alekseyev; "Stanislavsky" was the name of a Polish vaudeville performer), and embrace a despised profession.

Stanislavsky's obsession with "theatrical truth" grew and changed over the next forty years.

His axiom was to attempt to "Bring to the Stage the Life of the Human Soul" and, like many other artists, his attempts became more and more formal as he tried to codify his gains in knowledge, up until the point where they started becoming more and more mystical. He started out extending the set off the stage, so that the actor would not have to be shocked by the transition from the "real" into the "artificial," and, at the end of his career, he had his company sitting in a circle and endeavoring to transmit *prana*, or rays of energy, to each other.

All his work was to the one end: to bring to the stage the life of the Soul. As his vision of that life changed, he discarded the old and moved on.

The active life of even the most healthy theatrical enterprise seems to me to be, at most, ten years, and more probably, five to seven years.

The Company is an organism, and usually an organism made up of artists of at least slightly disparate ages.

The economic, social, and spiritual ties which bind a company aged twenty-five to thirty-five together will not hold those same folk at age thirty-five to forty-five. There are other reasons for the dissolution of the Company, but this one alone is sufficient.

The successful Company is only the manifestation of the successful artistic vision. When the Artist (in this case, the aggregated Artists, the Company) moves on, the dross, the "school," the physical plant, the administrators, the audience, stays behind, and, rightfully, demands that which they have been receiving for the last while. The Artists, however, are now constitutionally incapable of providing that same vision.

Two things may happen. The first, of course, is the disappearance of that artistic entity entirely. Equally possible and, in fact, more probable—in direct relation to the community acceptance of the Company—is the continuation of the *form* of the Company's vision with its content, and there we have the mechanics of the creation of a "school" of theatrical design, of playwriting, of acting.

In the 1930s, representatives of the very vital Group Theatre in New York (themselves descendants and offshoots of the Yiddish Theater) went to Paris to meet with a very aged Stanislavsky and discuss his "system" of acting. They returned to the States with an inspiration, an "outline" of The Stanislavsky System, and, significantly, their own place in the Apostolic Succession.

Many of the members of the Group Theatre had actually studied with members of Stanislavsky's Moscow Art Theatre, with Maria Ouspenskaya, and with Richard Boleslavsky, and others.

Boleslavsky's book *"Acting":The First Six Lessons* was and is a beautiful and useful anecdotal rendering of the Stanislavsky System. The true anointing of the Group, however, came with the direct Laying on of Hands by Stanislavsky in Paris.

The creators of the Group were the real possessors of theatrical insight, talent, and desire. These helped them to found a Theater; their anointing by Stanislavsky helped them to form a Gospel; and, since they had personally received wisdom from the Fount, it was they *alone* who could "create new bishops," who could anoint, who could bless, who might determine which work was correct and which was heresy.

The good and the bad of the Group Theatre, of any theater, is assimilated into and dies with the memory of the immediate theatrical audience.

The life of a Gospel, however, is somewhat different, and somewhat longer, as there is no immediate test of its utility; the received wisdom is not being judged and changed or discarded on the basis of its ability "to do the job," it has become an end in itself, it becomes a *creed*. The intellectual content of a creed is not to be used to aid its members in the wider universe, but, rather, their subscription to that content is to be used as a test to enforce their loyalty.

The point was not whether or not there were Communists in the State Department, or if there were, what damage, if any, they might have done; the point was whether one was willing to subscribe to the *assertion* that there were Communists in the State Department, and having done so, to eradicate, *not* those Communists, but, rather, all those who did not share the belief in their existence. So, the more blatantly incorrect or foolish the content of a creed, the more useful it is as a test of loyalty, for we may then be assured that its subscribers have not coincidentally accepted it because of its utility.

Similarly, with the Method—the philosophy/technique/aesthetic born in the Group and nurtured in the actor's studio—generations of actors, directors, and those who aspired to join their ranks, were informed, or inferred, that theatrical wisdom was available from a single fount, and that admittance *to* that source of wisdom was available only to those who swore allegiance, *not* to the idea of *Theater* (whatever the individual held that idea to be), but, rather, to the idea of the Method, an intellectual system *so correct* that its utility was not to be gauged by traditional theatrical tests, i.e., the ability of the performer to communicate the idea of the play to the audience.

The Gospel, received by the Group from Stanislavsky, was so successful—for Stanislavsky's ideas were and are very useful—that it outlived the brilliant artistic life of the Group, and survived in its institutional form as the Actors' Studio and the Lee Strasberg Theater Institute, at both of which we see the students of the students of the students of . . . to the seventh or eighth generation . . . Stanislavsky reiterating a series of theatrical notions in the creation of which they had no part and the actual utility of which they have never had to test before The Audience.

What those people possess is the honest faith that the things they have been told are correct. What they have lost is interest in whether or not those things are useful.

The overwhelming excitement at the birth of any new artistic experience comes from the sense of *discovery*, the sense that one is an explorer, and that, armed with nothing but a sense of humility and a healthy arrogance, one is creating something out of nothing at all. That one's tool, subject, and material is only the *nature of things as they are*. This cannot be found through reference to an authority.

Stanislavsky was driven to observe, question, and codify his theatrical thoughts to one end only: to bring to the stage the life, as he said, "of the Human Soul"; said life expressed not only and, perhaps, not even primarily, through the soul of the actor, but expressed through the soul *of the play*. So striving, Stanislavsky wrote, taught, and acted those things he found correct for himself and his audience, in that brief moment of time in which they lived.

Similarly, any truly creative artist living at any time and in any circumstances, is going to be moved or driven to observe the world prima facie, and draw those conclusions which will help him or her better to prosecute their Art. This observation will most probably include, but need not be limited to, nor even primarily derived from, instruction.

What is the answer to Stanislavsky's Bearer Bonds problem? Stanislavsky said that when one knew how to correctly analyze and perform the problem, one would know how to act; so, then, the question is, How Does One Act?

You start with a conundrum. You have to find the answer yourself.

A PARTY FOR
MICKEY MOUSE

I remember Riverview. This vast amusement Park was located on Chicago's North Side. It was magnificent, dangerous, and thrilling. There were freak shows, there was the renowned BOB'S roller coaster, the fastest in the world; there was the ROTOR, a room-sized cylinder in which one stood back against the wall and was spun around, while the floor dropped away; there was the PARACHUTE JUMP, the symbol of Riverview, and visible for a mile.

There was illicit gambling, one could die on the rides, the place reeked of sex. A trip to Riverview was more than a thrill, it was a dangerous dream adventure for the children and for their parents.

My father took me up in the Parachute Jump. We were

slowly hoisted ten stories in the air, seated on a rickety board, and held in place by a frayed rope. We reached the top of the scaffold, the parachute dropped, the seat dropped out from under us, and my father said under his breath: "Jesus Christ, we're both going to die here."

I remember wondering why I was not terrified by his fear. I think I was proud to be sharing such a grown-up experience with him.

Black men in jump suits sat suspended over tubs of water. White men paid to throw baseballs at a target. When the target was hit, the black men were dropped into the tubs below. The black men Uncle-Tommed in thick Southern accents.

The fix was in. Everyone was getting fleeced *and* short-changed to boot at the ten-in-one. Hell, that's why we *came* here. This was a *carnival*, this wasn't a merry-go-round and cotton candy, this was a *carnival*, and we were making fun of the horror of existence, saying, "Fuck *you*, tonight I'm going to *party*." And this was our Family Entertainment.

Did it bring the family together? You bet it did. And thirty-five years later I prize the memories. As does every other kid who went there with his family. As does everyone who ever went there, *period*. You got the bang for your buck that you were promised. Riverview; the very *name* is magic, to a kid from those days in Chicago; as magic as the name of the first girl you ever laid, and that's the truth.

My family took me to Disneyland the first year it was opened. I was eight, the year was 1955, and it seems to me that much of the park was still under construction.

I came back with my five-year-old, thirty years later. And

I remembered it all. I remembered the route from one ride to the next. I remembered where the hot-dog stands were. Nothing had changed. I was charmed to remember the Pirate menus in the restaurant, and how one punched out the ears of the menus, and could wear them as masks. I remembered the souvenirs. I went on the Dumbo Ride, and my wife took a picture of me and my kid, and it looks just like the picture of me and my mom on the same elephant.

Leaving the park, we ran into a parade on the Main Street of Disneyland. The parade was commemorative of the Sixtieth Anniversary of Mickey Mouse. The parade was a lavish panegyric, was designed to evoke feelings of fealty.

A part of the parade was musical variations of the Mickey Mouse Song: "M-I-C—see you real soon—K-E-Y . . . why? Because we *like* you . . ." et cetera; which song I both heard and sang along with weekdays for the several years I watched *The Mickey Mouse Club* on television. I remembered Jimmy Dodd, the *compère* of the Club, singing to us viewers, rather sententiously, and I remembered being moved by his affectation.

Well, here we were, kids and adults alike, smiling at that same Anthem, wishing Mickey well, thirty years later.

But I asked myself, what *actually* were we endorsing? What *was* it that we were wishing well? How, and to what end, was this warm feeling evoked?

Were we feeling "good" about wishing Happy Birthday to a mouse? It's not a mouse, it's a character in a cartoon. Were we wishing well to a commercial enterprise? For surely Disneyland is the most commercial of enterprises. It is the *State of the Art* in crowd control; it is terrifying to reflect that one stands in line for approximately fifty-five minutes out of every hour on a moderately crowded day at the park, that a five-hour sojourn at the park contains twenty-five minutes of "fun." The turns and bends and sights in the waiting line are designed to create the illusion that the line is shorter than it actually is. One sets one's sights and hopes on a Crest Up Ahead, which, surely, must be the entrance to the ride, only to find, on reaching that crest, that yet another stretch of waiting is in store, that one must wait, further, until one passes under the arches up ahead, certainly not too long a time. But on *reaching* those arches, one finds, et cetera.

Why does no one complain? Why does everyone return? Are the rides that thrilling? No, they are enjoyable, and some are rather good, but they aren't any more thrilling than the run-of-the-mill traveling carnival rides. Is the atmosphere that enjoyable? No. I think, to the contrary, that the atmosphere is rather oppressive. It is racially and socially homogeneous, which may, to a large extent, be a function of its geographical reality. But there is, more importantly, a slight atmosphere of *oppression* in the park. There is the nagging feeling that one is being watched.

And, of course, one *is* being watched. One is being watched by those interested in crowd control, both to extract the utmost in dollars from the visitors, and, also, to ensure their safety. The atmosphere and oppression come, I think, from this: that the park's concern for extraction far outstrips the concern for safety, but the regimentation is presented, as, foremost and finally, a desire to *care for* the visitor—to protect, to guide, to soothe.

One creates for oneself the idea that things at Disneyland

are being done *for one's own good*. And, far beyond obeying the rather plentiful signs forbidding one or another thing, one finds oneself wondering, "I wonder if this is allowed here . . ." "This" being, for example, smoking, eating-in-line, et cetera.

At Disneyland one creates (with a great deal of help) the idea that Every Thing Not Required Is Forbidden. And so we see, as in any other totalitarian state, the internalization of authority, and its transformation into a Sense of Right.

We see the creation of a social Superego, which is sometimes a handy tool, but perhaps out of place at an amusement park. I.e., (1) the Id says: "Well, hell, I'm going to Cut in Line, and get to Space Mountain sooner"; (2) the Ego says: "Don't *do* it, They will get you and, in some way, punish you"; and so, to overcome the anxiety and humiliation of being subject to a superior force, (3) the Superego is created and says: "No, it is not that you are *afraid* of authority, not at all, you are just concerned with Right and Wrong, and *you* want to go to the back of the line because it is the correct thing to do."

And it is *this* feeling that one is celebrating, I think, in singing paeans to Mickey Mouse, the feeling that I am a Good Person. I am one of the good, and *happy*, people, and I would never do anything wrong. It is this feeling that is being sold in the park. As an amusement park, it just ain't worth the money—far from being Riverview, it's not as much fun as a video arcade. The Mickey Mouse phenomenon is compelling not in spite of, but because of, its authoritarian aspect.

A cow was born on a farm near my home in Vermont.

We saw its picture in the local paper. The cow was notable for this: On its white side was found that conjunction of three black circles internationally recognized as the silhouette of Mickey Mouse. The mouse silhouette was rather large, perhaps three feet across, and was perfect. Mention was made that representatives of Disneyland were coming to look at the cow.

I later saw a news item to the effect that the park had purchased and was displaying this wondrous cow, and that only a fair retail price had been paid for the creature.

My first thought was, "Well, that's as it should be." And then I thought, "*Wait* a second. What is going *on* here? That blankety-blank cow is worth a vast fortune to the Disney folks." As of course it *is*, and I wondered, on sober reflection (1) why in the world the cow's owner would consider parting with the beast for less than a vast fortune; (2) why the Disney people would find a value in advertising that they (from another, and rather defensible point of view) *stole* this cow; and (3) why I was going along with their plan, and endorsing not only their purchase, but their proud announcement *of what they elected* was the "right" thing to do.

The Disney people were telling me that in paying only a "fair market price," or words to that effect, *they were protecting my interests.* Absolutely. That's what they were doing, and that's how I took it. How? In what possible way were my interests being protected?

The Disney people bought the freak cow for its publicity value. It was going to *create income* for their Company. *If* the cow were going to bring enjoyment to the visitors to the park (and, so, income to the Company), in what way would that enjoyment be affected by the price which the Disney Company paid for the cow? Is it not in the best interests of show business, on the contrary, to proclaim, "Brought to You at Great Expense"?

Why was I asked to be an accomplice, finally, to a lie? What was I being sold? Not "entertainment," not "amusement," not "a thrill." I was being sold the idea that I am a Good, Right-Thinking Person.

Well, I am capable of my own estimation of my own worth, and I don't need to be sold such an idea; and, difficult as it is, and it *is* rather difficult, I find that I have to admit that I don't like Disneyland. I think it is exceeding the job description for an amusement park to sell its product by appealing to, perhaps, even, by finally questioning, the self-esteem of the people who are paying the freight. There *is* no Mickey Mouse; and as to "Why, because we *like* you!," I'll be the judge of that, and thank you very much.

IN THE
COMPANY
OF MEN

It is not, I think, very energy efficient to have two parts of a machine performing the same task. A mechanical, and by extension, a spiritual, union might better be described as the conjunction of dissimilar parts such that the ability of each to realize a common goal is improved.

The roof is pitched to shed the snow, the floor is flat for the convenience of the occupants: Both conduce to the comfort of the inhabitants and to the structural integrity of the house.

Well, then, let's *talk* about sexual relationships. Let's talk about men and women. Our sexual organs, as has been noted, are dissimilar. It is also widely known, though to aver it in certain circles is impolite, that our emotional make-ups are quite different; and try as one may to hew to the Correct Liberal Political Line of Equal Rights, and elaborate a moral imperative into a prescriptive psychological view (i.e., Men and Women are entitled to the same things, therefore they must *want* the same things), we know that such a view is not true. We know that men and women do *not* want the same things (as much as they may want the *rights* to want and to pursue the same things). And *why* men and women want dissimilar things is, as they say, beyond the scope of this inquiry.

As I amble, so pugnaciously, into my twilight years and into what I so dearly hope will be a time of reflection and peace, it seems to me that women want men to be men.

This is a new idea to me. In my quite misguided youth, I believed what the quite misguided women of my age said when they told me and my fellows that what was required for a Happy Union was a man who was, in all things, save plumbing, more or less a woman.

Leisurely reflection would have revealed to me and the boys that women do not, on the whole, get *along* with women, and that efforts by men to be more *like* women would give those *actual* women yet another batch of objects with which to indulge in the, forgive me, intrafemale activities of invidious comparison, secrecy, and stealth.

So there we men were as, *disons le mot*, Dagwood Bumstead, and wondering why both we and our women were vaguely discontented without being in the least starry-eyed.

Well, then, for the moment, to hell with women; and to hell with the Battle of the Sexes, and its current and least charming aspect of litigiousness.

C'est magnifique, mais ce n'est pas la guerre.

Men get together under three circumstances.

Men get together to do business. Doing business is not devoid of fun. It gives us a sense of purpose. We run around in ways the society-at-large has determined are basically harmless, and, every so often, we get a paycheck for doing so.

Men also get together to bitch. We say, "What does she *want?*" And we piss and moan, and take comfort in the fact that our fellows will, at some point, reveal that, yes, *they* are weaklings, too, and there's no shame in it. This is the *true* masculine equivalent of "being sensitive." No, we are *not* sensitive to women, but we are sensitive to our own pain, and can recognize it in our fellows. What a world.

The final way in which men get together is for That Fun Which Dare Not Speak Its Name, and which has been given the unhappy tag "male bonding."

Now, let's talk turkey for a moment. Let's look at this phrase. What does it mean? We know, first of all, that it is not a description of a legitimate good time, and that "male" seems to be a derogatory modifier of an activity which in itself seems to be either an approximation or a substitution.

For, *who*, friends, do we know, who would suggest that we all spend a nice afternoon "bonding." What is "bonding"? It means this: it means the tentative and somewhat ludicrous reachings towards each other of individuals who are neither prepared to stand on their own emotional feet, nor ready, for whatever reasons, to avow their homosexuality. And if I'm lying, I'm flying. "Male bonding" is an odious phrase meant to describe an odious activity.

What *ever* happened to "hanging out"? What happened to "spending time with the boys"? What happened to The Lodge, Hunting, Fishing, Sports in general, Poker, Boys Night Out?

What happened to men having *fun* with each other? Because we do, though we may have forgotten, have quite a good time with each other, in the above-mentioned and other activities, and, though the talk is many, and perhaps, most, times of *women*, the meaning of the talk is: isn't it great being here together? Now, perhaps one might think this is latent homosexuality. If so, so what? And if you're sufficiently liberal as to hold that overt homosexuality is No Crime, then perhaps you might extend your largess to its latent counterpart, and, perhaps, further, we might look at our impulse to brand The Need of Men to Be Together with various types of opprobrium and just say, It's All Right.

Because it is all right.

It's good to be in an environment where one is understood, where one is not judged, where one is not expected to perform—because there is room in Male Society for the novice and the expert; room for all, in the Poker Game, the Golf Outing, the Sunday Watching Football; and room and encouragement for all who wholeheartedly endorse the worth of the activity. That is the true benefit of being in the Company of Men. And the absence of this feeling of peace, "Maybe she will think it's silly," is one of the most disquieting and sad things which a man can feel with a woman: It means "Maybe I'm no good."

I have engaged in many male, and specifically masculine, activities—shooting, hunting, gambling, boxing, to name a few. I have sought them out and enjoy them all vastly. They are times that I cherish.

I was sitting last October, bone cold, with some old-timers in a hunting shack, and they were passing around ginger brandy to pour into the coffee, and reminiscing about the cockfights which their dads used to take them to back before World War I. Is this corny? You're goddamned right it is, and I wouldn't trade it for anything. Nor the hanging-out at Mike's Rainbow Cafe, rest in peace, with a bunch of cab-drivers and bitching about the Police; nor leaning on the ropes and watching two guys sparring while a trainer or two yells at them; nor twenty-five years of poker games, going home flush, going home clean; nor doping the form out before the first race.

I love hanging out at the gunshop and the hardware store. Am I a traitor to the Cause? I have no cause. I am a card-carrying member of the A.C.L.U. *and* the N.R.A., and I never signed up to be sensitive.

In the Company of Men, this adage seems to operate: You will be greeted on the basis of your actions: no one will inquire into your sincerity, your history, or your views, if you do not choose to share them. We, the men, are here engaged in this specific activity, and your willingness to participate in the effort of the group will admit you.

Yes, these activities *are* a form of love. And many times, over the years, I have felt, at three or four o'clock in the morning, sitting out a hand in the middle of, perhaps, a vicious game, I have felt that *beyond* the fierce competition, there was an atmosphere of *being involved* in a *communal* activity—that by *sitting there*, we, these men, were, perhaps upholding, perhaps ratifying, perhaps creating or re-creating some important aspect of our community.

You may ask what it was about our passing money back and forth which was important to the community. And I am not sure that I know, but I know I felt it. And I know that it's quite different from business, and from the competition of business, which is most times prosecuted for the benefit of ourself as breadwinner, as provider, as paterfamilias, as vestigial and outmoded as you may feel those roles to be.

I was shooting partridge, and I watched the dog on point in the, yes, frosty morning, and I said to the other fellow: "Isn't that beautiful?" and he said, "That's what it's all about," and it certainly was. That day's shooting was about things being beautiful. And the trainer saying, "You got no friends in the ring," was about things being true, like the one player who says, "Don't call, I've got you beat," and the other one who pushes his stack in and says, "Well, then, I guess I'm just going to have to lose."

Is this male companionship about the quest for grace? Yes, it is. But not the quest for a mythical grace, or for its specious limitations. This joy of male companionship is a quest for and can be an experience of *true* grace, and transcendent of the rational and, so, more approximate to the real nature of the world.

For the true nature of the world, as between men and women, is sex, and any other relationship between us is either an elaboration, or an avoidance. And the true nature of the world, as between men, is, I think, community of effort directed towards the outside world, directed to subdue, to understand, or to wonder or to withstand together, the truth of the world.

I was sitting at a bar in Chicago many years ago. It was late at night and I was drinking a drink. An old waitress came over to me and correctly guessed the root of what she correctly took to be my state of the blues. "Look around you," she said. "You have more in common with any man in this room than with the women you'll ever be closest to in your life."

Perhaps. But in any case, to be in the Company of Men is, to me, a nonelective aspect of a healthy life. I don't think your wife is going to give you anecdotal information about the nature of the Universe. And perhaps if you are getting out of the house, you may be sufficiently renewed or inspired that she will cease to wonder whether or not you are *sensitive*: perhaps she will begin to find you interesting.

CORRUPTION

In his response to the Tower report, President Reagan said: The record *seems* to say that I traded arms for hostages, but in my heart I did not.

If we reduce this statement to meaningful English, we are left with this: "Whatever the report says is irrelevant—far from being bound by the report's findings on my actions, I am not even to be held accountable *for the actions themselves*—I am accountable only to 'my heart.' " I.e.: "*I* believe in my superiority to the public, to the law, even to the laws of logical discourse. *I* know what I was doing, and that's got to be sufficient for you below."

This behavior is an expression of the ultimate contempt for the electorate, the ultimate corruption, the megalomania brought about by power. Political corruption in the pursuit of money is limited by the location and the amount of the money; political corruption in pursuit of a personal vision of the public good is limited by nothing at all, and ends in murder and chaos, as it did in Nazi Germany, and as it does today in Central America.

Psychologically, the corrupt leader creates, and then offers himself as the only protection against, chaos. This is a ploy which recalls and recapitulates the experience of the unhappy child—the child forced to idolize the manipulative parent.

The corrupt parent says: "If you wish to be protected you must withhold all judgment, powers of interpretation, and individual initiative. *I* will explain to you what things mean, and how to act in every situation. There are no universal laws you are competent to divine or to understand—there is no understanding except through me."

So, Reagan's monstrous statement that he did not trade hostages in his own heart is an appeal to the child in each of us. It is, in effect, this threat: "If you want to remain a child, if you want to enjoy the privilege of life without fear, do not judge me. If you deign to judge me, I will withhold my protection." The corrupted person, politician, parent, doctor, and artist offer us two choices: to accept them and their presumption of power *totally,* or to reject them *totally* and, so, realize that we have been cruelly duped and accept the humiliation, anger, and despair that realization entails.

Those of us who have been in a position of authority as parents, teachers, employers, et cetera, know that it is often difficult to abide by our contracts with those over whom we hold authority. It is sometimes hard to remember that that authority was awarded to be exercised within specific limits, and not as an expression of unthinking and eternal fealty.

Those of us who have held authority know how great the temptation is to supersede our limits, to act "in the best interests of those under us," to, in effect, betray them for their own good.

In a normal lifetime we may have executed or experienced this betrayal; we may have spanked children, or humiliated students, or lied to those in our care—and while we were committing those corrupt acts, may have assured ourselves that we were acting for some higher good.

But most of us have also been on the receiving end of misused authority, have been spanked, or humiliated, or lied to, and we know that there is no good, no boon to be gained, no lesson to be learned from someone who treats us with contempt, who misuses a position of power over us.

The other night I was telling a bedtime story to my young daughter, letting my mind ramble and create a fantasy. As I neared the end of the story, I found myself beginning to weave in a moral—to cajole the free fantasy into having a "meaning" to reduce it to a motto. Later that night I thought about a phrase of Carl Jung's I had read some time before. Jung wrote that the analyst must enter into the fantasy/neurosis/dream of the patient.

I had, previously, found that phrase an expression of nice, human, common sense—a good but technically useless idea. As I reflected on my temptation to insert the moral in the fantasy, however, to make a freely told story about "bears" become, in effect, an advertisement for "safety," I felt uneasy. I felt that I had, "in my child's best interests," stolen her time to serve the purposes of my own agenda; and this gave me a clue to Jung's real meaning.

Jung meant, I believe, this: that it is *specifically* the renunciation, on the part of the analyst, of *the desire to control* that gives to the patient *and* the doctor the self-respect and strength to participate in the therapeutic interchange.

Now, analytic technique, philosophy, and method are, of course, essential; but without the act of self-renunciation by which the analyst ratifies the patient's position, they will not get a chance to come into play.

It is the renunciation *itself*, the act of respect *by* authority for its dependents, which is the first, *and the most powerful* good to be done for the patient; for, finally, the patient must cure himself; just as, finally, the country must rule itself.

As the analyst enters into the patient's fantasy (i.e., again, relinquishes the desire to control) whatever strengths, insights, and ideas he may have are relegated to a position *secondary* to his endorsement of the needs of the patient to express, and secondary to an endorsement and ratification of their contract. The patient will feel the renunciation in direct proportion to the effort which it cost the analyst. The patient, in effect, will have witnessed an act of *courage* performed in his interest. This act, an act of self-effacement, of deference, of respect, creates order. It is the opposite of the act of corruption, which creates fear.

If the bedtime story has political content—"and, so, the children came out of the woods, and they had learned never to disobey their grandmother"—the child may ostensibly seem reassured and comforted, but will, more deeply and importantly, feel rightly betrayed, for the parent will have misused a position of power and acted against the child's interest, and the child will take away from the story *not* the information and guidance it supposedly contains, but the more powerful idea: that the parent wishes to direct and exercise control in areas which are inappropriate; that the parent will not relinquish his or her power in favor of the child's rightful need for self-esteem. It is not important what was "in the parent's heart," what is important is that he or she thought the *dictates* of that heart more worthy than the legitimate interests of the child.

The bad parent says, "*I* will be the judge of what you need, not only are you going to be deprived, but I expect you to be grateful to me for my efforts to deprive you."

It is the same mechanism as "playing the Red Card." The corrupt politician says: "I, *alone*, am in possession of information heretofore unknown to you. This information is so powerful, you are in such immediate and pressing danger, that all laws and orderly methods of communication must be suspended, and *I alone* will decide what measures you must take."

It is the demagoguery of the third-rate politician, of the third-rate doctor: Believe me and live, or doubt me and die.

The same mechanism operates in the Theater. Only when the artist renounces the desire to control the audience will he or she find true communication with the audience—not power *over* them, but power *with* them.

Just as in politics, there is, in the arts, corruption which misuses the audience's trust in order to gain money (writing "down" to the audience) and there is corruption "in the audience's best interest": i.e., plays, productions, performances whose intention is to *change*, to *motivate*, even to *inform*.

The desire on the part of the artist to inform, to change, to motivate, may be laudable, but it is inappropriate in the theatrical setting. The audience has come to engage in *drama,* and before they rule on the truth or utility of the artist's "ideas," they will be affronted and disappointed by the inability of the artists *into whose care they have voluntarily placed themselves* to subjugate their own interests to the interest of their charges, the audience.

The director may set *Macbeth* in El Salvador; the playgoer may say: "How fascinating," but, subconsciously he feels affronted, and feels, "Who is this director to be teaching me a lesson and why does he see his *insight* 'the situation in El Salvador is not unlike the situation in *Macbeth*' as more important than his responsibility to me and to Shakespeare to tell the story simply?" (And if there are parallels between the situation in El Salvador and the plot of *Macbeth,* surely the viewer is as capable of perceiving them as was the director.)

The power of a person to serve is in direct proportion to the strength of his or her resistance to the urge to control. To possess or not to possess the urge to control others is not in our power—we may have it or not, it may come suddenly upon us with an increase in our "status" or supposed "power." To choose whether or not to *act* on such an urge *is* within our power. The man or woman in a position of authority who forgoes the inappropriate desire to control will stand not as a *message,* but as an *example* of strength, self-denial, and love; that example has the power to make our lives easier and ourselves less fearful; that example of strength endorses our desires for both autonomy and love, and serves as a balm for our pain in the pursuit of these sometimes divergent goals.

But the person who breaks the rules we have, as individuals or as a culture, created for interpersonal dealings (therapeutic, dramatic, familial, political); the person who sets him or herself "above the common," who is not willing to renounce the desire to control others, who cannot rid him or herself of the idea that he or she is acting "for the best reasons in the world," and so can exceed the authority ceded, does great harm.

We may, indeed, idolize that parent, doctor, teacher, leader; in fact, we generally do. We frequently need to idolize those who oppress us—the alternative is to feel the constant pain of their betrayal. The tyrant strikes a silent bargain with the tyrannized: "Identify with me, obey me unthinkingly, and I will provide for you this invaluable service: I will tell no one how worthless you are."

We idolize these people in inverse proportion to the extent that we believe in them. We respect and love, however, those who act as part of the community, who respect and love their fellows sufficiently to abide by their commitments to us and renounce their desire to control.

That Reagan cried at Bitburg, that he cries when the Holocaust is mentioned, that his heart tells him he did not trade arms for hostages—these assertions are none of our business, and a self-respecting man would forgo sharing them with us. They are equal to the parent who beats his child and tells him, "This hurts me more than it hurts you."

It is always the person in the superior position who says, "I am not laughing at you, I am laughing *with* you"; and always the inferior who knows this means, "I am both laughing at you and lying to you."

A COMMUNITY
OF GROUPS

Since the beginning of
Bob Sickenger's theater
at Hull House in the
early sixties, Chicago Theater has been a community not of
aspirants, but of citizens. Its progress and development from
beginnings at Jane Addams Center through the early days of
the Body Politic, Kingston Mines, and the heyday of Lincoln
Avenue, and to the present has been the progress of *groups*—
of individuals dedicated to the progress of a performance
group.

This has created a certain security in the individual members of the theatrical community (or at least the great possibility of such), and marks a difference between the theatrical
community in Chicago and that in New York. In Chicago,
the individual worker is striving to improve him or herself

and perfect his or her craft in the view of and for the benefit of a small group sympathetic to his or her aims (the company), rather than a large and unsympathetic group capable of perceivingly only results (the theater-going public and commercial production interests acting as their docents).

We in Chicago are, perhaps, therefore not enthralled with the question of *alienation*—of *identity*. A basic need of the worker has been met, and this enables him or her (represented by the *group*) to turn the attention outward, to concern themselves with the life of the city.

We, to a large extent, are chauvinists. We perceive the city not as an adversary, or as a random arena, but, quite accurately, as an extension of our dream-life. This is also an identifying characteristic of the Midwestern artist, who labors to explain to him or herself the *fact* of Chicago—understanding it as a manifestation of him or herself. E.g.: *The Pit, Sister Carrie, An American Tragedy, Lucy Gayheart, The Man with the Golden Arm, Herzog, Bleacher Bums, The Wonderful Ice Cream Suit, Boss, Some Kind of Life?, All I Want, Sexual Perversity, Grease, Working,* etc.

As citizens—which is to say as individuals who are secure in their own worth—we have been able to direct energy outward—towards expression and *actualization*, rather than towards merchandising, consolidation, and packaging. This freedom from puerile concerns has resulted in great growth, great vitality, and much artistic creation.

The theater has been forming, and reforming, on both geographical and artistic lines. Last year's church-sheltered improvisation is next year's institution.

The last fifteen years have seen the growth of the idea of

the strength and primary importance of the groups of individuals banded together with a common aesthetic aim; this idea has changed—in the general consciousness—from a nice but, realistically, impractical notion, and is now considered the necessary norm.

This is a great achievement, and creates the possibility of great achievement.

We in Chicago are proud of our theatrical workers in the same way Naples is proud of its singers or Washington State of its apples, if I may: "Yes, we grow these here—rather nice, don't you think?"

SOME RANDOM
THOUGHTS

TWENTY-FIFTH ANNIVERSARY

ISSUE OF *BACKSTAGE* (1985)

In 1960 I was bar mitz-
vahed. Nothing much
else of importance happened to me until 1963.

In 1963 I was working backstage at *Second City* and heard
Fred Willard introduce a scene by saying, "Let's take a sleigh
ride through the snow-covered forests of Entertainment."

That was my first personal encounter with Greatness, and
at that moment I knew that I owed it to myself not to become,
in the tradition of my family, a labor lawyer. My first true
milestone in the Professional Theater came in 1967. I had
been an usher and then the house manager at the Sullivan
Street Playhouse in New York. At that moment they happened to be doing *The Fantasticks*. One day the Assistant
Stage Manager got sick, and I was pressed into service running

the lightboard. In those pre-microchip days we had actual dimmerboards with huge dials and knobs and sticks, and some of the light changes involved plugging, turning, adjusting, replugging, etc., in sequences that were quite balletic.

My first and only night running the lightboard clipped along quite merrily until the end of the show. All the contestants on stage were reunited, El Gallo said, "So, remember: . . .," which was to be followed by a reprise of the song "Try to Remember." It was also my cue to do the most elaborate "send 'em home smiling" light change in Greenwich Village. Ever an innovator, however, I elbowed the master switch and plunged the stage, the house, and the light booth into total darkness for a period which can only be described as a "long, long time."

In the eighteen ensuing years not much has happened. Once, greatly depressed, and in New Haven (but I repeat myself), I was walking up and down in front of the Yale Rep. An old woman came up to me and said, "God bless you: You are the Savior of the American Theater, I have been to see your play six times." I cheered up and thanked her for raising me out of my self-involved, ridiculous torpor. I told her she had given me hope and that, yes, I was going to go home and write. I thanked her again. "Not at all, Mr. Durang," she replied.

In 1976 Dick Clark told me that Theater was all very well and good, but that, finally, it was "a flea on the ass of an elephant."

That's my report.

LIBERTY

In Hemingway's *A Farewell to Arms*, an American soldier, fleeing from the War, is playing billiards with a European Nobleman. The Nobleman comments that America will surely win the War, and the American asks him how he can be so sure. America will win, the man responds, because she is a young nation, and the young nations always win the wars. Then how is it that those young nations fade, the American asks, and he is told that they fade because they, with the passage of time, become old.

I once saw a film which recorded the transformation of an individual from arrogance to humility in the twinkling of an eye. An investigative reporter for a Chicago television station had hidden a camera to capture the dealings of a pimp who was brutalizing the young women who worked for him.

The Chicago police force had an undercover officer pose as a prostitute wanting to be taken on by this pimp. In the film she presents herself and the pimp struts and proclaims his dominance. To emphasize a point, he strikes the police-woman in the face and she falls. Several Chicago police officers appear from their hiding places, and for several very long seconds, beat the pimp summarily. The pimp falls to the ground and is immediately hauled back to his feet. He is broken and bleeding, and his arrogance is gone. It has been replaced by the demeanor of a child. "What has hap-pened to me," his eyes say. "It's only me, whom everybody *loves* . . . why are these people hurting me? Will nobody *help* me???"

Both the pimp's arrogance and its price are revealed to him in one moment. He becomes, in one moment, the perfection of the Tragic Form: he gains self-knowledge at the same moment that his state is transformed from King to Beggar—like Oedipus Rex, like Lear, like any nation which has grown old.

In our denial of asylum to Central American Refugees, we are avowing our state as an Old Nation—a nation resting on its laurels, a nation which draws its self-esteem from a bank of moral credit which, if it ever existed, was expended long ago.

"We need not *do* good," we are saying, "because we *are* good. Everybody *loves* us, and the things which we do are de facto good. They are good because we *do* them."

In our name, our Government asks, "How can we be sure these refugees are truly fleeing Political Oppression? What if they're just *hungry?* We will extend our sanctuary to the miserable to the extent they gratify our image of ourselves. As to their actual *need*, however, we do not feel we should be responsible."

And so a young nation's love of liberty has become a love of the power to control through the awarding or withholding of liberty. A love of liberty has become a love of power.

But in Emma Lazarus's poem, "The New Colossus," one hundred years old, we find not a love of power, but a celebration of humility before God.

Her poem and Bartholdi's statue of *Liberty* are a celebration not of blessedness, but of thanks. It was the act of a young nation to bless the hand of a God which had given it freedom to worship, to speak, to make a living. The Nation of 1886 thanked God in word and deed, and the deed was a happy sacrifice, and the sacrifice was open immigration.

In acceptance of the Stranger, in acceptance of the wretched of the world, America, the Young Nation, grew and prospered and became, in the inevitable course of time, an Old Nation.

We see the trappings of our age around us: an economy based on waste, the moral and economic cost of maintaining a standing army, immigration policies used as a political tool. These signs are both symbol and a further cause of the fear in the midst of which we live.

We look around and ask why we can no longer win a war, balance a budget, ensure the safety of our citizens at home or abroad. "Are we not," we ask, "the same good-hearted good-willed," in effect, "lovable people we have always been? Are we not still beloved of God?" And as we ask we are brought low by humiliation after inevitable humiliation. These blows are inevitable because, as per the laws of tragedy, our story is not yet complete. We are undergoing reversal of our situation, but we are far from recognizing it. We suffer at home and abroad because we are like the spoiled children of the Rich. We see comfort as our given state and we expect obedience from those we, on no evidence whatever, think of as our beneficiaries.

To ensure the safety of our self-image as Peacemaker, we have become a warmonger nation dedicated to the proliferation of arms: and we would, quite literally, rather die than *examine*, let alone alter, our image of ourselves as just, all-seeing, always right. So we, like the heroes of tragedy, like the pimp in the news film, have tried to appropriate to ourselves the attributes of God, and, no less than those other misguided heroes, we must and will and do suffer.

One hundred years ago, in a time of plenty of all kinds, in a time of spiritual abundance symbolized by Ms. Lazarus's poem and Mr. Bartholdi's statue, we were a different land. We were a Young Nation. Our National Conceit was not to be protector, but to be the comforter of the world. Our constituency was not the politically correct, but the politically repugnant of the world. And that office and that conceit and direction made us, for a time, a truly great nation.

In 1886, free open immigration offered America neither economic nor psychological hardship, today it would offer us both. And it would also offer us a peace and a protection not afforded by any nuclear arsenal or metal detector. Open immigration, as Ms. Lazarus pointed out, would give us something that would be both more comforting and more powerful than the strength of moral right, it would give us humility before God.

A SPEECH FOR MICHAEL DUKAKIS

I am not very much of
a political person. I be-
lieve most politicians
are No Better Than They Should Be. But I am saddened by
the decay of the American Political Process as most clearly
evidenced in the absence of true free debate between the
candidates.

It is not that I think that we ever had an honest presentation
of opposed ideas for the edification of an information-hungry
electorate, no. I do not long for an apocryphal Golden Age
of Symposia. I miss the political debate as a Vicious Brawl.
I miss the spectacle of the candidate using wit as a bludgeon,
and employing the tools of rhetoric spontaneously and with
no regard for the truth, in order to gain personal advantage.

What passes for political debate is, in these days, nothing

more than Trial By Ordeal. We, the electorate, score the fight on how perfectly the talking head can get through his set piece and detract points not for his inability to respond, but, on the contrary, for his inability to stick to the prepared text.

I was watching the first television debate between George Bush and Michael Dukakis. Being an American myself, I was waiting for one of the fellows to emerge as a clear underdog, so that I could root for him.

My hopes for a divertingly dramatic confrontation rose when Mr. Bush started assailing Mr. Dukakis's patriotism. "Well," I thought, "aren't his keepers *bold*, but won't they be disappointed when Dukakis comes back and *starts fighting dirty* himself!" "Yes," I thought, "now that Bush has 'opened the Ball' we're going to have an American Showdown. Oh Good." You, gentle reader, cannot only imagine, but probably shared my disappointment when Mr. Dukakis refused to Stand on his Hind Legs and Fight.

□——□

His pacifism offended my sense of both drama and history. Not only was it a chance for a good fight, it was a chance for a good fight in the great American Tradition of "Waaal, I have, as you have all seen, held my peace until now. And I have evidenced forbearance in the face of provocation, but Call Me Other Than a Man if I can keep still any longer!"

This is the *true* stuff of the American Dream: a peace-loving man given *so much provocation* that the very tenets of pacifism *themselves* would be offended if he did not come out and fight. (I call your attention to two of our major documents on the subject: *Shane* and *Bad Day at Black Rock*.) But Mr. Dukakis had not been paying enough attention to our cinematic heritage, and he retired to his corner irked when he should have been out there taking names.

So I, watching the television, became offended on the part of the viewership, and wrote Mr. Dukakis a speech, which follows here.

□———□

You know, every Presidential Election, one or the other side says that "never before have the choices been so clear, never before has the choice been so important."

Well, I don't know. A candidate, and those working for a candidate, like to feel important, we all like to feel important, and we each like to feel that our vote is important.

I don't know that this is the "most momentous choice you will ever have to make." But I think it is an important choice.

The election, as you see, has been hotly contested. I think it's *good* for the country. I think it's good to call things by their right name, and I see no reason not to.

Mr. Bush has implied, time and again, that I am not patriotic enough for him. Why would he say that?

He doesn't truly believe that I'm not patriotic. Why would he make such a charge?

He did it because it suited his purposes.

He doesn't believe that anyone who opposes the Pledge of Allegiance in the schools is not Patriotic. He says it because it suits his purposes.

He makes these slurs because I, as his opponent, *got in his way*, and it suits his purposes to abuse me, and to make

□———□

accusations that he knows are false. He did it because he found it convenient. He has also questioned my "passion."

What about "passion"?

What does a person care about?

Let me ask you a question.

Suppose you were at a party, or some social gathering. The conversation turned to the problem of the Homeless. You said, "There are so many more homeless in our streets today than there were ten years ago. What can we do?" You and your friends discuss the problem. One says, "Let's collect clothing," one says, "I wonder where we can send money or food . . ." and so on. . . . One man said "Let's create a thousand points of light."

What would you think about that man? He may be passionate about that *phrase*, but he's not passionate about the problem. If he were passionate about it, he would *do* something about it.

A pretty phrase created by some speechwriter is not passion. Passion is what a man or woman cares about. And you can fairly well judge what they care about by what they *do*.

What does Bush care about?

He cares about the special interests of himself and his group of cronies. He cares about them more than he cares about the Law.

He and his group subverted the Constitution, they subverted the Law of the Land, the Law they swore to uphold, when they traded arms for hostages.

For whatever reason they did it, they broke the Law, and they are unrepentant.

And you know it's true.

They aren't sorry they broke it, they don't even seem aware that what they did was wrong.

Now, you may, some of you may *concur* with Bush's actions, with the actions of his little group, *but be assured, that if he broke the law in THIS instance, which you may agree with, he will break the law, and bend the law, and look the other way in other instances with which you DISAGREE, and to purposes which you find despicable, as soon as it suits his purposes.*

You may have remarked his use of the phrase, "The Governor of Massachusetts." And the constant references to my being from Massachusetts, as a sort of "code."

His inference is that, "You know and *I* know that Massachusetts is, somehow, not part of America," or "*less* than American," or not part of the "America" of which you and I approve.

Does Bush believe this?

Does he actually and "passionately" believe these snide remarks and insinuations, that one part of the country is less worthy than another?

Of course not. He's an Easterner, he spent much of his life in Massachusetts, he went to school there. That's who he is.

And what sort of a man would stoop to divide the Union of these United States through insinuation and sarcasm?

Why would he do that? He knows that Massachusetts is neither less nor more American than any of the other states.

Why would he disparage his own heritage? Why would he imply something he knows is unjust, and untrue, in addition to being destructive?

He did it because it suited his purposes.

And if he did it when it suited his purposes about *my* State, he will do it, when it suits him, about the State in which *you* live, or the Union to which you belong, or the profession which you practice.

You can listen to the voice which says, "What do you expect from the Governor of Massachusetts," and you can hear the same voice saying, "What do you expect from a steelworker," or "from a doctor," or "from a Southwesterner."

And many of you feel "included" by his, in effect, "winking" at you, by these coded references that seem to say "You and I know who the good and the bad people are . . ." (Pause)

Well, we all like to feel included. I personally don't believe there are "good and bad" people. *But I do believe there are good and bad ACTS.* And I believe it's a bad act for a public official to break the law *for WHATEVER reason,* and I believe it is a bad act for a public official to curry favor through lies, through half-truths, and through insinuation. *There is no REASON to divide this country.* And the public forum should concern itself with what *unites* us.

A lot of mystery and ceremony has become associated with this job of President.

It's an important job, and, in confusing times, we sometimes look for the person who holds this job to be all things to all people.

And, so, the election process itself has become, year by year, less of a reasoned casting of votes, and more, if you will, of a "beauty contest."

The man who can say the right catch phrase first, the man

who can best master "the use of the camera," the man who is the next-to-the-last to get caught out in some mistake or inconsistency gets awarded the prize.

But the job was designed, and the job should *be*, to *preside*, to preside over legitimately opposed factions in such a way as to *represent the interests of the people as a whole.* To represent their interests, as expressed in our laws. And, especially in these momentous times, amidst crises of health, of foreign relations, of the environment, of human necessity, that is what the job must be.

Now, I am not a passionless man; it is not my nature. But I believe that the job of Chief Executive should be performed, and is performed best, by a man who is *not* a zealot; who refers his decisions to the rule of Law, always in the knowledge that he was elected *not to enact his own whims*, his own "passions," but to represent his constituents; and to put the rule of law, and the will of the People *as expressed in Law*, above his own will.

If elected, I swear to obey the Laws of this Country, and to tolerate *no one* in my administration who subverts those Laws.

I swear to work for *all* the people, for the people from *all* our States; for the homeless, for all minorities, for those oppressed by hardship, and by illness.

This is a remarkable time in our history.

We can look at the vast changes around us with Fear, but we do not *have* to be fearful.

We can, as a Nation, take a deep breath, and say that we are *equal* to those changes. And we *are* equal to them.

There is not a challenge, whether it is housing, or World Peace, or AIDS, or the budget, which we, *working together*, are not equal to.

We can be nostalgic for the Past, but the Past is gone, and nothing will bring it back.

This is a time of change, and, for good and ill, the Past is behind us.

With it, we have lost segregation, the oppression of Women, and of Labor, and countless other social ills. We have started to put them behind us.

We have also lost the comfort of World Peace, of a stable economy, of a clean environment, of a country safe from the ravages of disease. But *these* things can be reclaimed.

They can absolutely be reclaimed. By a populace working together, undivided, working together under the Law.

It is that populace I was raised to be a citizen of, and it is that populace of which I want to be President.

I am asking you for your vote. Thank you.

□——□

That's the speech. I sent it to his People by a mutual friend. He never used it; and if *any* of you readers might be inclined, even fleetingly, to think, "Why, hell, if that man had just said those words, he'd be President today," I would, of course, most humbly demur, and respond, "Oh, hell, I was just trying to even up the fight . . ."

A FIRST-TIME
FILM DIRECTOR

I started writing screen-plays in 1978 (*The Postman Always Rings Twice*).

Along with most other screenwriters and Other Ranks, I quickly conceived a desire to direct movies. My agent told me that the best way to break into that job was this: write an original screenplay and hope someone wants it badly enough to bet on you as a director.

Michael Hausman, producer of *Amadeus, Ragtime, Heartland*, etc., liked the screenplay and gave me the chance to direct it, which I did. We filmed the movie the summer of 1986 in Seattle. It's called *House of Games*, it stars Lindsay Crouse and Joe Mantegna. It's a *film noir*, psychological thriller.

Here is the story:

A psychiatrist (Crouse) treats compulsive gamblers, drinkers, etc. One of her patients tells her that he is $25,000 in debt to the Mob, and if he doesn't pay within the week, he is going to be killed. The patient pleads with her to intercede. She goes to the gamblers who hold the patient's marker. She becomes involved with one of them (Mantegna).

He is, by profession, a confidence man. Crouse, fascinated by the man and his life style, starts going out on criminal escapades with him; she becomes more and more involved.

Here are some thoughts on directing my first movie.

FAMILIAR AND

NONFAMILIAR OCCUPATIONS

I once had to take a specific dose of pills with me on a trip. I shook the pills out of the bottle, counted them carefully, tore a sheet of paper out of my notebook, wrote the dose and directions on the sheet, and poured the pills onto the sheet and twisted it into a spill, an action from a pharmacy of a bygone day.

As I did this, I was overcome with a sense of *déjà vu.* "I have *absolutely* done this before," I thought.

This was a feeling I never had while directing the film.

It seemed to me, prior to attempting the job, that film directing was like barn raising: the job was laid out, the opposing walls would be hoisted up, and the farmer would scramble up a ladder to peg the opposing walls together. If the farmer had not done his job correctly, he would be left fifty feet in the air, leaning against an unsupported wall, with the people who employed him and the people he employed standing down below and watching his shame.

I'd written for the movies before, worked with the directors, and been around a set. It was obvious to me that there were many aspects to the job, that I was good at some of them, competent at others, and at a complete loss in several of the most important. In those areas in which I have no talent and little understanding, it occurred to me, I had better have either a good plan or a good excuse.

The area of which I was completely ignorant was, unfortunately, the visual. Oh well, I thought, and went back to hit the books.

I decided that I was going to plan out the whole movie, shot by shot, according to my understanding of the theories of Sergei Eisenstein.

I found Eisenstein's theories particularly refreshing, as they didn't seem to call for any visual talent. The shot, he said, not only *need* not, but *must* not be evocative. The shot should stand as one unemotional term of a sequence, the totality of which should create in the mind of the audience a new idea, e.g., rather than the shot of a distraught woman crying, or the same woman describing to her friend over the telephone how she found out her husband was cheating on her, Eisenstein would suggest the following: (1) shot of woman reading a note; (2) shot of the note which reads, "Honey, I'll be home late tonight. Going bowling, I love you"; (3) shot of woman putting down the note, looking down at something on the floor; (4) her point of view, shot of the bowling ball in the bowling ball bag.

In the example above, each of the shots is uninflected and unemotional and so the shots could be determined by someone without visual "talent," but who knew the "meaning" of the sequence, i.e., a woman discovers her husband is cheating on her.

So I thought, Well, that's for me; I'm not going to be John Ford or Akira Kurosawa, but I *do* know the meaning of each of the sequences, having written them, and if I can reduce the meaning of each of the sequences to a series of shots, each of them clean and uninflected (i.e., not necessitating further narration), then the movie will "work"; the audience will understand the story through the medium of pictures, and the movie will be as good or bad as the story I wrote.

That was the task I set myself in preparation: to reduce the script, a fairly verbal psychological thriller, to a *silent movie*. It seemed to be a tough, and possibly pointless, task, but I've always been more comfortable sinking while clutching a good theory than swimming with an ugly fact.

So I made out the shotlist, then I tried to sketch the shotlist in a bunch of cunning little rectangles, each representing what the shot would look like on the screen. Then I arrived in Seattle to make the movie.

PREPRODUCTION

Three people were in the production office in Seattle. Somebody went to Abercrombie & Fitch and got their deluxe Pigeon Shoot dart game. We played Pigeon Shoot for much of the first few days. We drove around and scouted locations,

I wrote letters to friends back home. "This is a breeze," I thought. Then everybody showed up.

As a kid I did a lot of white-water canoeing. Once, up in Michigan, I was in the stern, shooting some rapids, when we hit a bad rock broadside and swamped. The canoe with me in it was pinned upside down in the white water, and the force of the water was such that I couldn't get out. "I'd be okay," I thought, "if someone would just turn this thing off." And so it was when the movie got rolling.

Our producer had to put together "the board," that is, the schedule of what gets shot when; the production designer had questions about the color of a wall; the costume designer wanted to go out shopping; the propmaster wanted to know how many poker chips of which color were needed; the transportation captain, et cetera. Now: this was the kind of action I was looking forward to. I like to make decisions, and I like to be at the center of things, but this was a bit too much of a good thing. Everybody said that the prime requirement for a film director was good health, and I quickly saw the reason. *Each* decision is important. *Each* decision is going to affect the film. *Each* choice presented to you is the result of work and thought and concern on the part of the person asking the question. Sloppiness won't do, and petulance won't do. Also, I *prayed* for the chance to direct a movie, nothing would do but to do the job, which I was fast realizing was, in the main, administrative.

So I got the job in hand and tried to remember to meditate twice a day, and preproduction was going along pretty well. Then we started with the Real storyboard.

The Real storyboard was going to be drawn by our professional storyboard artist, Jeff Ballsmeier. It was to be, in effect, a comic book of the entire movie, showing what the camera was to shoot, where the camera was to move.

Ballsmeier and I and our cinematographer, Juan Ruiz-Anchia started meeting to transform *my* storyboard into The storyboard.

The only trouble with my original efforts was that all my drawings looked like amoebas, and that those things they represented "would not cut" (i.e., could not be assembled into a coherent film).

CROSSING THE LINE

And so, as Stanislavsky would say periodically to his students: "Congratulations, you have reached the next step of your education."

The storyboard conferences were incredibly exhausting for me. I had to force myself to think in totally new concepts. Most of these concepts were on the order of "How many boxes are hidden in this pile?" and it was like taking a visual intelligence test for several hours every day, with the questions written in a foreign language.

In cutting film, the *axis* of the shot, I learned, has to be preserved. If the hero enters looking to his *left* at the heroine, then, in subsequent shots, he has to *continue* looking to his left. You can't cut to a close-up and see him looking to his *right*. *Unless* . . . and here followed a list of Talmudic exceptions which I could never follow, but which Jeff and Juan discussed quite a bit, while I felt *very* stupid.

One is not supposed to *cut in axis,* i.e., from a longshot of a subject to a *closer* shot of the same subject or vice versa, unless . . . et cetera.

When trying to show *passage of time,* one had better not cut from the subject to the same subject again *unless . . .*

All these rules are to this point: *Don't confuse the viewer.* I tried and tried, and the editor, Trudy Ship, showed up and said don't worry, it will become clearer when you're in the editing process. The next one will be easier. *(Insh'allah)* And so we went on making up the shotlist, the conference room was covered with diagrams, the table was covered with sketches. Juan and I and Jeff would posture and pace around the room saying things to each other like, "Okay: I'm the ashtray and you're the camera," and getting very excited. It felt like the Algonquin Round Table on Speed.

My days of preproduction were like this. I would go from a costume fitting, to a storyboard conference, to a location scout, and driving back to my apartment, I hit the same tree three nights in a row. I would arrive home, thank God I hadn't fallen asleep on the way, take my foot off the brake and start out of the car, and the car, which was still in drive, would proceed into the tree.

The numbers on the days-till-shoot notice on the office wall got lower and lower. The cast showed up for rehearsal. We were all Old Cronies, and had worked together on the stage, most of us, for at least a decade, and had a happy reunion in Seattle. Rehearsals went swimmingly, and it was just about time to shoot.

Full of beans, and happy in the flush of having convinced somebody to let me direct a film, I said to myself: Think past the shooting process. Plan the film, and always think towards the *editing*. The script, for good or ill, is finished, and it's going to work; you have wonderful actors, you have a superb D.P., don't go out there on the set to "improvise," or even to "create," but, simply, *to stick to the plan*. If the plan is good and the script is good, the movie will cut together well and the audiences will enjoy the story. If the plan is *no* good, or the script is *no* good, then being brilliant or "inventive" on the set isn't going to be to much avail. In effect, *keep it simple, stupid*.

Well, those were fine words, and very comforting to me, and I put up a great front and ate a lot of fresh Seattle salmon with the cast and crew, and preproduction went on apace.

Always a cocky lad, I had told the producer not to worry about me as a first-time director—that he would get either a good film or a sincere apology. The night before the first shot, my jollity came back to haunt me and I had a *crise de foi*. I couldn't sleep, I got the shakes, "I can't *do* this," I thought, "who in the *world* am I fooling?" And I wallowed in self-pity and fear for a while, until the words of the great Dan Beard came to me: "Just because you're lost," he said, "don't think your compass is broken." And then I was, for that moment, suffused with Peace. I wasn't taxed, I saw, with having to make a masterpiece. Whether or not the movie was even any *good* was, at this point (on the night before shooting), fairly well out of my hands, all *I* had to do was stick to the plan. "Hell I can do *that*," I thought, "all I've got to be is obstinate." So I went to sleep.

The husbanding of energy in directing a movie is, I found, of as much importance as the husbanding of time: there's only so much of it, and you don't want to get into deficit spending.

Mike Hausman produced *House of Games*. His favorite axiom hangs on a sampler in a prominent position wherever his command post is. It reads: ALL MISTAKES ARE MADE IN PREPRODUCTION.

I was happy I made the amount of film decisions I did in preproduction, because when the snowball started rolling downhill I could barely remember what the movie was about, let alone try to think where to put the camera.

THE SHOOT

We had forty-nine scenes and forty-nine days to do them in. We had to average approximately two and a half pages a day (about average). We had about twelve hours a day to get those two and a half pages.

Each day Juan and I and Christine Wilson, the script supervisor, would meet with Ned Dowd, the first assistant director (the man who ran the set), and reduce the storyboard to a list of shots, e.g., Scene Two: (1) a master of the entire action; (2) a close-up of the patient; (3) a close-up of Doctor Ford; (4) an insert of Ford's wristwatch; (5) a shot of Ford writing on a pad, etc.

We would plan to shoot in one direction as much as possible, so as not to have to relight twice, then turn the camera and shoot in the reverse direction. The average shot-list for each day was nine shots. And we would proceed in a deliberate and orderly fashion, cast and crew, from one shot to the next, and then go home and fall into what I wish

I could describe as a dreamless sleep, but which comes closer to a "night of fitful musings." (I should point out things would proceed in an "orderly fashion" until the end of the shoot, when I, "smelling the barn," as it were, began to lose it, a bit, and wish that everything could happen all at once so I could get dressed and go to the Opening.)

My job, once the shooting began, was a lot of worry, and a lot less work. Having started into the day's shotlist, I was fairly free from one shot to the next, and improved the hours by drinking tea, while our magnificent crew worked full-out dealing with the foreseen: the necessity of putting light places where it is not and taking it away from places where it is; and the unforeseen: cars that would not start, a mailbox that had to be removed, a prison elevator to which the key had been lost, a ruined costume, et cetera.

I was in constant awe of the crew, camera, light, and grips. Many friends and acquaintances had told me that a film director's life was taken up with professional intransigence of the crew and with time-wasting minutiae. My experience was completely the opposite. I felt that *these* guys were setting the example and that I was just along for the ride, and would (and did) do well to follow them. They were up all day, they were up all night, they were hanging lights on window ledges ten stories up, they spent the night in a crane in the rain.

They came over to ask me my opinion regularly, not because of any talent on my part, or because of any expertise I had demonstrated, but because the film is a hierarchy and it was my job *to do one part of it*: to provide an aesthetic overview, and to be able to express that overview in simple, practicable terms—more light on her face, *less* light on her face; the car in the background, *no* car in the background.

I came over to the camera once every hour or so to "approve" a shot the D.P. set up. My "approval" drill was this: go over to the camera, look through the lens at a brilliant clear composition which reflected the essential nature of the shot, thank the cinematographer, return to my camper.

Most of "approving the shot" made me a bit nervous. I understood the drill of deference, I understood that *someone* had to be in charge of the movie, and that someone was me, and that I was doing it; but I *did* feel like a great big interloper looking through the camera. One part I did like was turning my hat around. I wore a beaked hat throughout the shooting, and when I walked over to the camera I would drop my glasses off my face and turn my hat around, so that I could get close to the eyepiece. That was a never-failing source of enjoyment, and I felt great and I felt I *looked* great doing it. The hat was given to me by Dorothy Jeakins, the costume designer. She designed *The Postman Always Rings Twice* (1980), which was my first experience with the movies. And she had worked with Cecil B. De Mille, and told me the hat was from some De Mille extravaganza, I have forgotten which. I also rented a pair of jodhpurs to wear on my first day as a director.

My plan was to show up on the set in jodhpurs, a monocle, and my Dorothy Jeakins hat. On the way to the set, however, this costume struck me as a tad *chudspadik*, and so I, thank goodness, refrained. (I *did* put this directing drag on after finishing the first day's shooting, and posed in it with the actors on that day, Ms. Crouse and Ms. Kohlhaas.)

Mike Hausman, the film's producer, thoughtfully scheduled one easy 1½-page scene as the first day's work. So we finished that scene and another 2-page scene written for the same location, but scheduled for the *next* day, all in three hours and I ended my first day as a director, *one day ahead of schedule* (which was, of course, Mr. Hausman's secret plan) and I put on the jodhpurs and posed for a picture.

I didn't take too much of a deep breath until after the third day of shooting, when our first day's dailies came back from New York. I got drunk with my assistant, Mr. Zigler, and we poured ourselves from "The Thirteen Coins," a Seattle Bar and Grill, into the screening room, and there, sure enough, was the film we took on the first day. Juan's photography was beautiful, the acting was beautiful, it was going to cut together and make a movie.

There's an old joke about the belowstairs gossip on the night after the Prince and the Princess got married. "What happened?" says the butler. "Well," says the chambermaid, "the Prince comes in, the Princess says: 'I offer you my honor,' the Prince replies, 'I honor your offer.' " "And that's it?" says the butler. "Yep, that's about it," says the chambermaid, "all night long: honor, offer, honor, offer."

And that was about it for the shooting of the movie. Shoot, go home, shoot, go home, et cetera.

The previous September in New York, I was on a panel with Spike Lee, Alex Cox, Frank Perry, and Susan Seidelman. The topic of the panel was: Directors Discuss Independent Films. As questions were addressed to the other panelists, I listened and thought, enviously, "Gee, I wish *I* could be a film director." That's how it was on the set. Day by day we followed the plan. No "light at the end of the tunnel"—just getting the day's work done. At night we went to the dailies, and Juan and Mike Hausman and I sat in the back row with Trudy Ship, the editor, and I would look at the takes I asked to have printed and tell Trudy my preference, and in what order the shots could be tacked together to make the scene.

At the beginning of shooting, I printed only two takes of each shot. As the shooting went on and I got more and more fatigued, I started to print more and more takes. One day Mike Hausman suggested politely (and correctly) that I was "going native," and that I only had to print one or two; and if those were not sufficient, I could always print up the outtakes. Not only was he right economically, but, I noticed, he was right artistically.

As a screenwriter, I spent a bit of time watching others direct; as the husband of a film actress I spent more time doing the same. I would frequently ask myself: "*Why* is that guy shooting so much?" And the answer occurs to me now: he's probably tired.

There is a condition called hypothermia, and it occurs when the body can't keep itself warm. Two of the symptoms are inability to think clearly, and panic; and it's no joke, it happened to me once alone in the woods in winter and I was lost and very lucky to stumble across a road before I froze to death.

A situation very like this state of mind is brought about by stress as well as cold; and if Eisenstein would have lived longer and spent more time in Hollywood, he might have talked less about the Theory of Montage, and more about healthy eating, and what to have on the Craft Service Table.

Speaking of the theory of montage, it was very easy to choose between two takes of a shot. I found it difficult to choose among three and impossible to choose among more. As my fatigue led to vague anxiety, I had to remind myself more frequently to Stick to the Plan and Keep It Simple, Stupid: to follow the shotlist and storyboard in such a way as to capture the simple, uninflected shots which would cut together to make the movie.

How successful was this stoical approach? Well, it made the editing process very straightforward, for the most part. There were scenes which were superfluous, which had to come out; a few looks which were needed and were not shot and so had to be "stolen" from other shots or scenes, but, for the most part, the editing process, like the shooting process, was a reflection of the original plan of the storyboard.

The storyboard was, in effect, the "script" we were going out to shoot; and it is the prejudice and observation of a writer and theatergoer that, finally, the production is only as good as the script.

DO YOU WANT TO WORK OR

DO YOU WANT TO GAMBLE?

What did we do for fun on the set? Well, we did a whole bunch of things, and would have done more, except I am a rotten liar, and when we had planned a gag I'd be laughing so hard I couldn't say "Action," and so the object of the jokes, who was almost invariably Lindsay Crouse, would get wind that something was up.

My favorite was the Spawning Salmon. Crouse did a scene on a bench overlooking an embankment overlooking Elliott Bay. She's supposed to be staring out to sea, and we sent a production assistant down below the embankment. On cue, he was to heave this ten-pound salmon up into the air, where it lands at her feet. You can see it on the Joke Reel, but Crouse is staring a few degrees off to the side, and concentrating on her acting, and she didn't actually see the salmon. Ned Dowd instructed me that good form dictated that I tell the script supervisor that we should print that take because "there was something special at the beginning that I think I liked."

Ned Dowd won $56,000 off of me at blackjack, and I'm just lucky that he allowed me to cut double-or-nothing One Last Time several more times. Gambling was endemic in the cast and crew. One sequence of the film is a poker game, and many of us, for the week that sequence took, spent twelve hours a day in a staged poker game and the remaining twelve in a real one.

Crouse had an actor friend dress up in a bunny suit and prepare to hop through the back of a shot on her cue, but it seems that that day I was a tad "out of sorts," Crouse was reluctant to make my day harder, and so the actor stayed under the table we were shooting, dressed *en lapin* for four hours. We shot one long sequence in a pool hall, and spent a lot of time between setups shooting pool and learning trick shots from the pool hustlers, and so on, and there you have it. We were a cross between a mobile army corps, an office, and a bus-and-truck company; we were a happy family.

WHAT I REMEMBER

I remember shooting the film's last sequence on the last day of shooting. In the scene, Joe, one of the actors, is to get shot, and I remember his wife sitting behind the camera crying as she watched him do the various takes of his death scene.

I remember racing the dawn on a couple of weeks of night shooting; trying to get the last shot before the sun came up, and the seagulls cawing a half-hour before dawn. I remember our wonderful soundman, who wanted to break into acting and was given the part of a hotel clerk. He had to say, "May I help you?," and take a pen out of a penholder and a form off of a sheaf of forms, and hand them to Crouse and Mantegna. We drilled him on the specific timing of the movement of the pen and form, and told him that the whole rhythm of the shot keyed off of his precise movement; and then, on his first shot, we glued the pen into the holder and the forms together. I remember the camaraderie on the set—the sense that we were engaged in a legitimate enterprise as part of a legitimate industry, and that hard work and dedication would ensure one a place in the profession. I remember thinking how very sad that this feeling is absent from the Theater, where *no one* is guaranteed employment from one year to the next, where this year's star writer, actor, designer, may not work again for years; and I remember feeling grateful that I could feel that camaraderie again.

WHAT I'M GOING TO DO
DIFFERENTLY NEXT TIME

We finished shooting the movie on time and under budget in mid-August. I went home happy as a clam and immediately got as sick as I've ever been in my life. I couldn't get out of bed for two weeks, didn't eat a thing, and sweated the whole time. Sidney Lumet called to welcome us back. "How did the film go?" he asked my wife. She told him. "How's David?" he said. "Is he sick yet?"

Back in the editing room, Trudy Ship told me that, as I look at the film, I am going to think the following three things: I shot too much, I shot too little, I shot the wrong thing. This, basically, is what I *do* think as I look at the film. There is a lot of coverage I shot that was never used; the main cost of this is not the exposed film, or even the more serious lost setup time, but this: When capturing footage that is essential, the mood and the work on the set is, of course, more directed than when capturing footage that is protective. There is a lot I *should* have shot. There was one close-up I left out which necessitated a reshoot and wasted a lot of worker-hours. Finally, my Master Plan was not directing the movie, *I* was directing the movie, and next time out, I'll know more about what to shoot, what not to shoot, and when to deviate from the plan.

Next time I'll eat nothing but macrobiotic food, exercise every day, and, God willing, work with exactly the same people.

FILM IS A
COLLABORATIVE
BUSINESS

Working as a screen-
writer I always thought
that "Film is a collab-
orative business" only constituted half of the actual phrase.
From a screenwriter's point of view, the correct rendering
should be, "Film is a collaborative business: bend over."

When one works as a screenwriter, one is told that the job
is analogous to being a carpenter—that as much pride and
concern as one takes in one's work, one is only working for
hire, and the final decision must be made by the homeowner.

The analogy, I think, is not quite correct. Working as a
screenwriter-for-hire, one is in the employ *not* of the eventual
consumers (the audience, whose interests the honest writer
must have at heart), but of speculators, whose ambition,

many times, is not to please the eventual consumer, but to extort from him as much money as possible as quickly as possible. The antagonism between writer and producer is real and essential; and writers tend to deal with it by becoming enraged, leaving the business, or, by suiting up and joining in the game by exploiting the *producer* for as much money as possible.

But Man oh Manischevitz what a joy to be on a project which was *not* a "collaboration." In the summer of 1986, I directed a script I had written, *House of Games.*

As I write, we are in New York, at Transaudio Studio, and engaged in the last three days of the sound mix. After the sound mix, nothing remains to be done to *House of Games* except the color timing; and when I finish working on the color timing then the film will be completed; almost exactly one year to the day since the start of preproduction.

Here at the studio, the sound team and the film editors and I work from nine until six.

At six, the *House of Games* people leave, and the sound people from the *Untouchables* come in. I wrote the script for *Untouchables.*

We finished photography for *House of Games* on a Saturday in August, and *Untouchables* started shooting the following Monday. I had the fantasy of going to Chicago with a deck chair and a bottle of beer, and sitting behind Brian De Palma and watching him direct.

I didn't act on my fantasy. I flew from Seattle, where we were filming, to my home in Vermont, and got deathly sick and didn't get out of bed for two weeks.

Two very different experiences—*Untouchables* and *House of Games*: a big-budget and a low-budget movie, being the screenwriter and being the writer/director.

My experience as a screenwriter is this: a script usually gets worse from the first draft on; this may not be an immutable law of filmmaking, but in my experience it is generally true.

Untouchables may have been a bit of an exception. I met with Brian De Palma three or four times, and he and Art Linson, the film's producer, had some ideas for cuts and restructuring which definitely aided the script.

Inevitably, however, De Palma, Linson and I disagreed about several aspects of the film and, as usually happens, we got to the point where someone said to me: "Look, we disagree, and (in effect) you are the employee, so do *you* want to make the script changes which we require, or would you like us to do them, and do them badly?"

On films in the past, this mixture of flattery and aggressiveness usually brought me around, like other screenwriters, with a sigh to make the requested changes. On *Untouchables*, however, in the final and minor instances where I disagreed with the director and producer, I said fine, *you* fuck it up. Spare me.

I said the above for a number of reasons: (1) that I have gotten to the point as a writer where I am tired of being finessed; and (2) that I was directing my *own* movie, and had no sympathy to waste on the plight of others.

It is my experience that up to a certain point, somewhere around the submission of the first draft, a filmmaker's anxiety is dedicated to the script for want of other idleness, and that that anxiety is more or less on the level of "What am I going to wear to the prom?" Like that prom anxiety, the worry is not how to choose the correct outfit, but a handy mask for a basic feeling of unattractiveness and unworthiness.

When a film actually goes into production, however, the frantic phone calls about the script cease. In fact, once in production it is almost impossible to get a director to change a script on request from the writer—the script is a thing of the past, and the director is now worried, as he should be, about *the film*.

What *does* one worry about while directing a movie? This: "I've forgotten something." The time is ticking so quickly, and one is never going to get it back. The director thinks, "There's a shot that I forgot to take; there's a piece of business which pays off in reel eleven, and I've already shot reel eleven, and I think I just forgot to shoot the setup in reel two; I haven't left room for a cutting 'out' . . ." et cetera. One feels the constant pressure of time and thinks, "I've shot too much, I haven't shot enough, I've shot the wrong things."

I am very well acquainted with Creative Panic; and, over the years, have learned to deal with it as a writer, by using the *Lawrence of Arabia* approach: "Yes, it hurts, but the trick is not minding that it hurts."

As a writer, I've tried to train myself to go one *achievable* step at a time: to say, for example, *"Today* I don't have to be particularly inventive, all I have to be is *careful*, and make up an outline of the actual physical things the character does in Act One." And then, the following day to say, "Today I don't have to be careful. I already have this careful, literal outline, and all I have to do is be a little bit inventive," et cetera, et cetera.

Many people ask me if I write on a word processor. I write longhand, first, and then do subsequent drafts and corrections on a typewriter. I like to have all the actual physical pages that I have done in front of me: all the drafts, and all the revisions, and all the markings on them. It gives me a sense of security; i.e., "look at all these drafts you have done, you must be a very responsible person—now all you have to do is use your good taste and refine these pages."

When directing on stage, I would, similarly, arm myself with a detailed outline, the intentions of each character, and notes to myself on how to communicate these intentions to the actors (through means of direction) and to the audience (through manipulation of the scenic elements).

So, prior to directing *House of Games* I resolved, once again, to try to overcome my natural laziness, my natural aversion to tasks I would characterize as "routine," or "uncreative," and to apply myself to a series of detailed outlines: of the actions of the characters, of the rhythm of the movie as an expression of the proximity of the protagonist to her goal, and, finally, of the shots, shot by shot, of the entire film.

So that's what I did. Once again, I subscribed to my "mountain climbing" theory of creative endeavor—get an absolutely firm foothold, and then make a small excursion to another absolutely firm foothold.

Armed with my outlines (prior to photography) I thought this: You've *been* creative, in the writing of the script; you've been responsible and careful in the reduction of the script to shots and directions which you can communicate to the crew and cast; now all you have to be is courageous, and *stick to the program*; and that is what I tried to do.

House of Games is a very different movie from *Untouchables*. Our budget was modest and theirs was large; *Untouchables* has big-name stars, and ours does not; and *Untouchables* was made by an ad hoc group, while *House of Games* was made up of a group of friends and colleagues of long standing.

Someone once got the better of me in an important business dealing by what I thought was fairly sharp practice. I was pitying myself in this regard one day, and the friend with whom I was talking—a high-level film producer—said, "Forget it. Forgive and forget, you both are going to be in the business a long time, chalk it up to something, and go on."

This seemed and seems to me good advice, and I have never been able to take it.

Like all of us, I get my feelings hurt easily, and, like most of us, I have tried to learn to deal with it. As I grow older, I have begun to learn to forgive, but have never learned to forget.

Hollywood is the city of the modern gold rush, and money calls the turn. That is the first and last rule, as we know, of Hollywood—we permit ourselves to be treated like commodities in the hope that we may, one day, be treated like *valuable* commodities.

In accepting the brashness, and discourtesy, and inevitable cruelty of a world without friendship, we promote and strengthen that world. We all do it, and we do it either in resignation, or in the hope of subsequent gain. But none of us likes it; and when we cease to notice it, there's probably not much of the creative force left in us. How can you create if you think of yourself as humiliated and venal? Not very easily, and I speak from experience.

This is not to say, of course, that all transactions between strangers in Hollywood must come to grief. But I think somewhere between "many" and "most" of them do. So I thought that, on my first movie as a director, and, as what seemed to me a matter of good principle, I would stack the deck, and make the movie with my friends, actors and designers with whom I had worked for many years.

Another of my friends, Art Linson, was the producer of *Untouchables*. When we'd shoot the bull over the phone, me shooting in Seattle and him in preproduction in Chicago, he would say of some production problem he was having on his large movie, "You don't know how lucky you are . . ." But I did know.

I had worked with the five principal players an average of eleven and a half years apiece, I had worked with the two designers for ten years, and with the composer since we were kids in high school.

These people had no need to prove themselves to me, and, more important, I had no need to prove myself to them. That energy (small or large, but inevitable) that is devoted to establishing bona fides in an artistic collaboration between strangers ("How much does this other guy know? Can I trust him, is he going to hurt me?") was in our movie devoted to other things.

During the shooting of *House of Games* Art Linson flew from *Untouchables* preproduction in Chicago out to Seattle to meet with me about changes he and Brian De Palma wanted in the *Untouchables* script. I am afraid that my lack of helpfulness was tempered both by the necessary callousness of "just not having the time to concentrate on someone else's problems," and, if the truth be told, by at least a twinge of enjoyable cruelty; i.e., "You guys made me intermittently miserable for a couple of months, and I 'had to understand your position.' Now *you* understand mine. . . ."

I was probably also making Art and Brian pick up part of the tab for seven or eight years of work with producers who forgot to say "thank you," or used the phrase "moral dilemma." I was, in short, feeling my oats. I was strutting a bit after seven years on the receiving end.

There is that about film directing. The amount of deference with which one is treated is absolutely *awesome*. One is deferred to by the crew because of the legitimate necessity of the chain of command in this sort of an enterprise, and by a great deal of the outside world because of supposed and real abilities to bestow favors, contracts, jobs, orders, et cetera.

This deference was awfully refreshing after several years acquaintanceship with Hollywood in the position of a writer (where, I should point out, I was treated, if one wants to judge by local standards, exceedingly well).

One of my most treasured Hollywood interchanges follows: I made a suggestion to a producer and he responded, "The great respect that I have for your talent doesn't permit me to sit here and listen to you spout such bullshit."

It is nice to be treated with deference, and, I think, even nicer to be treated with courtesy; which, I think we can all say, is almost universally lacking in Hollywood transactions.

How often do we say, or think, "Yeah, I like you, and you like me, so we don't have to go through the garbage of being 'nice,' because we have a movie to make, and our crassness is not going to make the movie any worse." But, of course, it does make the movie worse; and even if it didn't, it makes the time spent a little less enjoyable.

Also this: I think we know that the callousness which passes for Refreshing Frankness in many Hollywood dealings doesn't exist as a direct way to expedite a difficult business—it exists, again, because we view each other as bargaining chips, and we tend to think thusly: "I can treat you any way I like, because, *if you need something from me*, you have no recourse, and I'm letting you know it." Correct me if I'm wrong.

The downside of all that jolly deference and courtesy one receives as a film director is, of course, that one has to *direct* the movie.

Directing is, I think, a lot like being a night watchman over something one finds personally priceless: one must be unstinting in vigilance over a very long period of time, and it *does* get draining.

When in my "Keep printing this shot until Kodak hollers Uncle" stage I'd sit watching the dailies with ten or twenty of the cast and crew, and, as I'd printed six takes and couldn't remember the first when I'd seen the sixth, I'd ask for hands on who liked which take best. . . . Every time I'd ask for a vote I'd get a few giggles, a few hands, and a lot of nervousness, and then it *came* to me that *I* was the director, and that it wasn't funny. The people in the cast and crew were working hard enough at *their* job and I shouldn't, even in jest, be asking them to do mine.

That's what I learned on my summer vacation.

Film is *not* a collaboration, which implies equality—if not of contribution, at least of position. Film is produced under the most stringent and detailed conditions of hierarchy, as we know. To pretend otherwise is to insult those lower on the hierarchical scale, and to excuse those higher on it. And I found that the highest courtesy one could enjoy or perform was doing one's own job well.

Personally, I found film directing grueling, exhilarating, sobering, and addictive. I loved it.

Art Linson tells me that Brian De Palma is going to let me see *Untouchables* next week, and I can't wait. Next week, also, I will, as I said, be, except for color timing, signed off of *House of Games*, and, several weeks after that, I start thinking about preproduction of my next movie with Mike Hausman, *Things Change*, which we start filming in October.

PRACTICAL PISTOL COMPETITION

Marksmanship appeals to two basic aspects of our American character: the love of skill, and the desire to hear things go boom.

I have been a backyard marksman (the more technical term is *plinker*) for years. I have a bull's-eye target set up on a stump twenty-five yards behind my back porch, and a bunch of swinging metal silhouette targets out beyond that; and, to break up an afternoon of writing or pretending to write, I periodically step out on the porch with a .22 pistol and plink away. My wife says she can "hear me thinking."

It is awfully enjoyable to be able to extend your reach fifty or sixty yards—to hear the metal silhouette go "ping," or to break the Necco wafer. To find enjoyment in handgunning, you have to be able to hit the target fairly regularly, and to do that you need to practice the basic skills. There are only two of them.

The first is correct trigger pull. It used to be said that what the shooter wanted to do was squeeze the trigger so that he would surprise himself when the gun went off. More accurately, however, what the shooter wants is this: *gradually* to take up the slack in the trigger (short of letting off the shot) while correctly aligning the shots so that when the pistol's sights are aligned in correct relation to the target, the last, least pressure on the trigger will let off the shot.

The second skill is obtaining correct sight picture. It is one of the bizarre anomalies of handgunning that one concentrates *not* on the target, but on the pistol's front sight. In shooting you are aligning the following: the target, and the pistol's front and rear sights. The rear sight is two and a half feet from your eye, the front sight is three to ten inches beyond that, and the target is seventy-five feet beyond *that*. There is no way all three can be kept in focus at once. So what the shooter does is let the rear sight *and* the target go slightly blurry, while keeping the front sight in sharp focus. When you can learn to do this, when, after long practice, you can force yourself to resist the natural impulse to look at the target, you begin, as if by magic, to hit what you are shooting at.

My eyes are terrible, but after a few days of good, correct practice, I can hit a quarter at twenty-five yards with some degree of regularity. (The quarter is actually a great target because, taped in the center of a black bull's-eye target, it offers great contrast. One of the most impressive and simplest demonstrations of marksmanship is shooting out a candle at night: it's awfully easy to line up your sights in the flame—it's the only thing you can see.)

The handgun was developed as a weapon of personal defense. Dating from the first practical multishot revolvers of Samuel Colt (1836), the handgun began to replace the saber in the cavalry charge and the cutlass in the naval boarding.

Skill with a handgun was, as we know, highly prized on the American frontier. In the twentieth century, as we Americans moved from the country to the cities, we had less need to develop skill in marksmanship; and the handgun, as one needs practice to shoot it well, ceased being regarded as an accurate weapon. General consensus was that with a pistol, "you shouldn't shoot at it if you can't spit on it."

The handgun began to acquire a reputation as an inaccurate weapon, useful for personal defense or offense, capable only of inflicting a terrible amount of damage at close range, and useless for any legitimate sporting purpose.

This attitude began to undergo a change after World War II, and this change was brought about by the F.B.I.

The F.B.I. observed that despite rigorous firearms training, its agents and law officers around the country were being killed and wounded in shootouts.

The F.B.I. agents, as all other police officers, and amateur handgun marksmen at the time, were being trained to shoot at bull's-eye targets at fixed distances. And the F.B.I. concluded that such training did not equip the agents with the skills necessary to come out on top in the less formal but more exacting competition of a real gunfight.

A practical course was developed to teach marksmanship as it applied to gunfighting.

The agents were trained to shoot at moving targets rather than stationary ones. They were trained to shoot quickly and accurately at unknown distances and from different postures and in different lights; to make quick and accurate shoot/ don't shoot decisions; to shoot from behind cover; and from unconventional postures; and while moving; to reload and clear malfunctions quickly—to do all these things under stress, not the stress of physical danger, but the stress of *competition*. Police forces around the country sent and still send members to the F.B.I. course to learn and return home to teach practical pistol skills.

In the 1950s, inter- and extradepartmental competitions developed to test these *practical* handgun skills. The handgun, viewed since the turn of the century as an inaccurate weapon of defense, became an accurate sporting arm to be used in marksmanship competition.

Various pistol sports developed: P.P.C. (Practical Pistol Competition), which stressed the basic police skills of target acquisition, quick decision-making, reloading, and marksmanship; I.P.S.C. (International Practical Shooting Confederation), which concentrated on those things in a rather more athletic way, and involves scaling obstacles, et cetera.

The bowling-pin shoot, a popular pistol event, awards the speed with which a marksman can draw and knock six bowling pins off a table at twenty-five feet. These sports stress the combination of speed and accuracy.

Silhouette shooting was imported from Mexico (*siluetas*

metálicas). This sport is devoted to extracting the ultimate in pistol accuracy, and it involves knocking down metal silhouettes of animals at distances to three hundred yards.

Hunting with the handgun as an alternative to the rifle became, and is still, popular.

In the late sixties, top competitive shooters began opening schools to teach handgunning either for sport or defensive purposes. Gunsmiths around the country began custom tuning and custom building pistols and revolvers for increased accuracy and competitive utility. And prestigious and lucrative pistol competitions—the Bianci Cup, the Soldier of Fortune, the Second Chance—attracted top competitors and much spectator interest, and so improved and continue to improve the breed. It might not be too much of a stretch to compare competitive handgunning to sculling—both sports have loyal and dedicated spectators and competitors; and very few besides these competitors and spectators know the sports exist.

Much of the I.P.S.C., P.P.C., and bowling-pin competition of today is done with what is generally known as a Colt .45 Auto. This is a semiautomatic pistol in .45 caliber, and is familiar, from the movies, even to nonwarriors.

The pistol was designed by John Browning for the Colt Firearms Company, and was adopted by the United States government as a sidearm in 1911. (The pistol was recently replaced by the Beretta 92SBF 9 mm.)

The patent was given by Colt to the United States government during World War I, and the pistol was made, and still is made, by many manufacturers in addition to Colt.

I found one of those manufacturers by accident in the back

of a health food store. I was buying something tasty, and heard heavy machinery noises coming from the next room. I asked and was informed that there was a gun factory in the basement. I went down and discovered the Caspian Arms Company of Hardwick, Vermont.

Caspian was making very high quality automatic pistols on contract for some highline American arms companies. They were also making a super accurate M1911 .45 pistol under their own name. The owner showed me targets shot offhand (without support) at twenty-five yards. All the shots were in one hole. This is both remarkable shooting and a *very* accurate pistol.

Next to the target was taped a schedule for the Vermont Handgunners Association (the existence of which I had not theretofore been aware). The schedule listed a P.P.C. meet coming up in one week in a town near me. I remarked that that sounded like fun and Cal Foster, the owner of Caspian Arms, remarked, "Why don't you go?" I told him I couldn't go as I didn't have a .45 automatic, and he suggested that I just borrow *his*, which is just what I did.

(To digress for a moment, and on the subject of Mr. Foster's generosity: Colonel Homer Wheeler, reflecting on his life on the frontier [*Buffalo Days and Ways*, 1925], wrote, "In countries where the populace is armed, men generally tend to be more polite.")

Mr. Foster loaned me his pistol and two magazines, so that I could compete. The pistol was fairly representative of what one does to transform a stock-as-a-stove firearm into a competitive one. The barrel is lengthened by one inch. The barrel is *ported* (i.e., ventilated) on the top of the protruding portion. Recoil tends to make the muzzle of a pistol rise after each shot. Gases escaping through the porting tend to counteract this rise and keep the muzzle down—thus making for faster on-target follow-up shots. The safety is ambidextrous, so that it can be safely manipulated when shooting either with the right or left hand. The trigger is tuned for a crisp, fairly light let-off. The pistol has high-grade adjustable sights. The magazine is believed to facilitate quicker insertion of a new mag. There are several other things done to the pistol, but those listed are the major ones.

In addition to spending amounts possibly in excess of a thousand dollars on his competition pistol, a serious competitor will invest in special competition belts and holsters, and will, most probably, load his own ammunition. (The last, in addition to offering the ability to tailor the cartridge to the competition, affords a great savings. Factory .45 ammunition costs around twenty dollars for fifty. Home-loaded ammunition can be one tenth that. It makes a difference if you're going to practice as a *truly* serious competitor would— with fifty thousand rounds a year.)

I took Cal Foster's competition pistol over to my backyard range and, after a very educational week, I was able to keep most of my shots on a shoebox at twenty-five yards. (The .45 is a bit more difficult to shoot well than a .22 target pistol. It is heavier, it is heavy over the hand, rather than at the muzzle end, it is, generally, not very forgiving. *You* have to learn to shoot *it*.)

I practiced reloading, shooting with the weak (in my case, the left) hand, drawing from the *surrender* position (both hands held shoulder high). I blithely went down to the P.P.C. meet at Benson, Vermont.

The Benson meet was divided into three parts: Assault, International Rapid Fire, and Shotgun. This was the order of the assault course: The shooter starts with his pistol holstered and both hands in a surrender position. On command, the shooter draws and fires two shots at a target twenty yards out. He then runs ten yards and, leaning out from behind a barricade, fires two shots at a target ten yards out. Continuing, he must fire two shots on each of two targets fifteen yards out. He then runs ten yards, kneels behind a barricade, and shoots twice at a target at twenty-five yards. He runs another ten yards, again kneels, puts two shots on a ten-yard target, and fires at a metal plate suspended five yards from him. The sound of the plate being struck stops the clock.

The shooter is scored on his time over the course, and on his point score. The target, like a bull's-eye target, is made up of concentric circles, and hits closest to the center score highest. Unlike a bull's-eye target, however, these scoring circles cannot be seen by the shooter, who must determine his point of aim and shoot to it without external signs. The targets are torso-sized cardboard cutouts. They are flanked and partially obscured by similar torsos, which are covered with an "X." Hits on these "hostages" accrue penalties to the shooter.

The man before me ran the course in 43 seconds and scored 121. He would have stopped the clock quicker, but his first shot on the metal stop plate went high. I thought, "How untutored of you—*don't* you know that when shooting

at targets beneath you, you must hold *low?*" My lack of charity
was soon to be rewarded. I ran it in 1 minute 43, and scored
89. I couldn't find my spare magazine in my belt; I reloaded
at the wrong time; I couldn't hit the stop plate at *all*, I couldn't
hit the target, I finished shaking like a leaf.

I looked forward to the International Rapid Fire Course:
simple timed fire at twenty-five yards. "Here," I thought,
"my backyard training is about to pay off." But I made the
same mistake as the F.B.I. In my backyard, I was training
for an event which I was good at, but at which I wasn't going
to be tested. My showing at international rapid fire was
wretched.

I assembled my gear and watched a state trooper fire the
assault course. He moved not at all slowly, but with complete
determination. He placed his shots right around the 10 ring,
and two inches apart. He reloaded at the right time. He was
obviously a man who had trained as if his life depended on
it, as, in his case, it did.

Driving back from the match I was a bit chagrined—not
because I did badly, but because I was silly enough to think
that I would do well. The essence of Practical Pistol Competition is *to shoot well under pressure,* and if I wanted to
develop that skill I would have to train *at that.* This thought
brought me back to marksmanship as a Stoic discipline.

It is easier to teach a woman to shoot a handgun than it
is to teach a man. A woman has fewer preconceptions, less
at stake, and is more willing to follow the first principle of
marksmanship: If you look at the front sight you hit the target;
if you look at the target, you waste your shot.

One of the most respected figures in handgunning is Bill

Jordan, ex-Marine marksman, ex-border patrolman, marksmanship demonstrator, gun writer.

Someone asked Mr. Jordan about the training of police officers: Isn't it impossible to *know*, they asked, what a man will do under pressure? Mr. Jordan replied that, far from impossible, it was the easiest thing in the world: "A man will do what he's trained to do."

This, to me, is the beauty of marksmanship: that it tests, under great pressure, those skills and principles we have developed in moments of calm.

It is possible to quickly "go native" and start upgrading your equipment: your leather, your reloaders, your pistol, your ammunition. Generally, though, the gun always shoots better than *you* do, and you're left with the basic first principles: (1) front sight, (2) squeeze, (3) practice. Follow those principles and the shot goes where you want it. The gun *does* go boom, and that's nice; but better than that is the feeling of having done something right.

WHEN
I WAS YOUNG —
A NOTE TO
ZOSIA AND WILLA

When I was young, the corner restaurant made a thing called a fran-cheezie, which is the best thing that I ever ate. It was a hot dog sliced down the middle, filled with cheese, wrapped in bacon, and then sizzled on an open grill until it snapped.

And at the pharmacy they made a drink called a Green River, made with green syrup and carbonated water; or root beer, or any kind of soda that you wanted.

My father always had a Chocolate Phosphate, which is a thing we had in Chicago. It was made with chocolate, carbonated water, and a secret ingredient.

It was so cool and seemed dark in the drugstore, and smelled of vanilla and chocolate, and like nothing else in the world.

Even the water there was special. It was served in a white cone upside down on a cool silver base. And in the summertime how cool that marble counter was when we had been out playing.

We played Kick the Can on summer evenings. Or we'd play ball in the streets, where the first manhole was a single, the second a double, so on down the street. And someone always watched out and yelled "Car."

There was a row of garages back on our alley, tied together under a flat roof that ran the whole block, and sometimes we'd climb up and play football on top of the garage.

The policeman on our block was named Tex, and he wore two stag-handled guns on his belt.

Times in the street, infrequently, there'd be a horse-drawn rag truck. The ragpicker either yelled, "Rags, Old Iron," or else that's something I remember from the stories my mother used to tell me of her old neighborhood.

I remember that we had an organ grinder and his monkey who would come around. And I remember Gypsies, though I don't remember how the Gypsies looked or what they did.

At school we'd line up, boys on one side of the building, girls on the other. When the whistle blew we would march in.

In eighth grade, I was a patrol boy. I wore a white belt and helped the crossing guard. There was a special way you learned to fold the patrol belt, and wore it clipped to your pants belt during the day. When it dropped below ten degrees in winter, they gave the patrol boys hot cocoa.

And I remember in the schoolyard every spring, the coming of the Duncan YoYo man, dressed in his Duncan YoYo costume, who would demonstrate the latest models and the latest moves, and was an artist of such skill we were not envious, but awed.

We had a School Store on the corner. Joe sold candles, pens and pencils and three-ring paper. Once he spied a shoplifter, and cursed at him, and moved his huge bulk out from where he sat behind the counter and he caught the shoplifter and shook him on the sidewalk until the candy fell out of his shirt and on the street.

On Saturdays I walked two blocks to the Theater, and, for a quarter, saw fifty cartoons and a movie, which was usually a Western, and I came back after dark.

Once they raffled off a bicycle and I think that I almost won.

I lay on my lawn in the springtime, on my back, and watched the winds blow high clean clouds over the lake.

My first friend told me that his father rode in a jeep in the War, and almost lost a foot when the jeep which they rode blew up.

Down the street a new family moved in. The man came by and borrowed money from all of the people on the block and never paid it back.

I learned to ride a bike. They say you never forget how; and I remember how it felt to learn. How it felt to be pedaling alone that first time, and I knew that it was going to hurt when I fell, and I didn't give a damn.

And we had the Park and the Beach and the Museum, and I don't remember why I wasn't killed when we would spend the day climbing around the museum caryatids thirty feet above the ground.

We lived near the railroad tracks on the South Suburban Line.

When we went downtown, we bought tickets from the old woman in the old wooden booth up on the platform.

The waiting room smelled of steam and piss and in the winter it was the warmest place on Earth.

They had black steam engines then, and when we waved at the engineers, they always waved back.

And now I'm older than my parents were when I was young.

The best thing since then, I think, is just being here with you.

ENCASED
BY TECHNOLOGY

The movies find them-
selves in between the
past and the future.
Their ancestor is, of course, the Theater; which required no
technology whatever, and is just a story told in a formalized
manner.

The movies' progeny are the electronic media, which require the work and the conspiracy of many thousands to
produce and to reclaim an image.

In a world without electronic circuitry, in a world without
electricity, a world which nuclear or natural disaster may very
well bring upon us, videotape will not be a medium for the
transfer of information, that videotape which exists will no
longer be translatable.

A radical but arguable thesis is that the progression from the acted drama and the printed word to a culture most of whose works are *erasable* is, perhaps, the cosmic reason for the existence of videotape. After The Bomb, after The Deluge, the record of our world will be erased and good riddance to bad rubbish. We see this progression at work in our daily lives already.

Microfiche, microfilm, and computer storage have virtually replaced the library as the repository of information.

Their care, operation, repair, etc., require increasingly more specialized and trained personnel. The writings, the thoughts of the culture are increasingly less accessible to the people, more prone to accidental erasure or alteration, more liable to the control, censorship, or inadvertence of both technocrats and government.

A man or woman may make a book or publish a pamphlet, may, in effect, disseminate their thoughts with little or no help or approval from the vast bureaucracies of government or industry, but the broadcasting of the electronic image, the manufacture and distribution of videotape, is in the hands of a group which grows smaller every day; and a person receiving a rejection from the networks or the distributors takes little comfort from the rejection being phrased, "We do not think this is commercially viable," rather than, "This is contrary to the wishes of the State."

The very image of videotape has been abstracted from human experience close to the point of nonrecognition, so that only the most superficial resemblances to the "real" exist.

In a theater we have our live fellows before us, acting out

stories. In film we have, wonderfully, a recreation of the very light which fell on them. In video we have that light reduced to electrons, and those electrons splayed upon a screen.

Like binomial numbers, the electrons do not handily communicate information which cannot be reduced to the statistical. They do not easily deal with the "suggested," with the approximate, with the ambiguous, in short, with Art.

Movies were the first new art form since the invention of painting. Acting has always been acting, and music still music whether live or recorded. Painting and drawing are essentially the same whether practiced on the stone of caves or on the stone for lithographs, or on canvas.

Movies are the first art to link the plastic and the temporal. They take place both tangibly, in the image, and continually, in the juxtaposition of those images. They find their ancestor only, perhaps, in the picture gallery, and the comic strip.

Video is another form altogether, and is linked more closely to the ticker tape. Video is the unceasing display of superficial information. (This may be why television has so rarely attained the status of an Art. It is linked not to the expression of the soul, but to the eventual and necessary regimentation of all thought. It is linked to the computer.)

But the art of Movies, as Eisenstein said, is the art of creating an image not *on the screen*, but in the mind of the beholder. (The juxtaposition of image A with image B creates in the viewer the thought C; e.g., a windlashed beach and a woman looking out of a window create the idea of apprehension.)

It is no accident that the birth of movies was coeval with the writings of Freud. At the same time Freud was saying "I understand the significance of dreams," Lumière et al. were beginning to put those dreams upon the screen. They were juxtaposing pictures to create an idea in the mind of the audience.

Movies represent the magnificence of the late Victorian Era, when it was thought possible for one man to "know all things," a phrase which embodies the magnificent misapprehension that knowledge is both finite and reducible to a technical expression, the *reductio ad absurdum* of which we see in video, where the concern for knowledge and its expression has been subsumed in the quest for technical expression devoid of content. I cite videographics.

The very ease of television production has hypnotized us all, as the speed of ticker-tape information accelerated the corruption of the stock market, and the speed of the auto has destroyed the commercial integrity of the American town.

These necessary, inevitable, and God-Willed accelerations which began at the turn of the century, created, in their first stage, the solace (at its best) and the morphia (at its usual worst) of the movies.

Our confusion with the accelerated world created the need of and the fact of the first new art form in fifty thousand years, the movies.

The movies stand between the past and the future, between human history and human extinction. They come into being at the beginning of the last stage of the Industrial Revolution, which is to say at the beginning of the End of the World.

In a technological age, our heros are not the prime movers, not the creators, but the agents, the conductors who take us safely through a journey. We lionize not the explorer, but the pilot, not the statesman, but the president, not the writer, but the director, not the architect, but the "developer"; we have elected to admire and envy that person who is encased by technology, that person whom we see as the *captain* of technology, who, rather than being crushed by the juggernaut, has, alone, mastered its controls.

These lavishly rewarded technocrats are adored for their supposed ability to conduct us through a dream, through an experience of both the plastic and the temporal. They are believed to possess the ability to, if you will, steer us through a dream, to assemble and order the universe through the medium of technology.

As a sometime movie director, I have had the experience of standing, encased by technology, between those two worlds of the past and the future, of dealing with the most ancient art of Drama in a medium requiring the assistance and compliance of several hundred people, of being, in effect, a pilot.

On the movie set you hear the beautiful cadence of a specialized workers' language. The cameraman says, "Lose the opal, please," and the gaffer shows him the image with and without the filter and says, softly, "Opal *in*, opal *out*, opal *in*, opal *out*." Or he shines more and then less light on the subject to be photographed, and announces, "Flooding, flooding, flooding, flooding; spotting, spotting, spotting, spotting."

The cadences sounded familiar to me—I knew I had heard similar rhythms before, and it occurred to me that I'd read them in *Life on the Mississippi*.

The lead man stood on the prow of the steamboat and heaved the lead and shouted, "Mark Twain, Quarter Twain,

Quarter *less* Twain . . . No bottom . . . ," and gave information to the riverboat pilot, who was the most lionized and
romantic representative of *his* time. He was elected to bend
a new technology to the whim of the people, and so conduct
them on a new journey.

The analogy to transportation is, I think, both curious and
appropriate.

In the last one hundred fifty years, those controllers of the
latest in transportation were enshrined as the heroes of the
day.

Canal pilots, steamboat captains, railroad engineers, avia-
tors, astronauts, those elected to guide the fastest, most dangerous, newest, and technologically most exacting means of
transport were, until their technology was superseded, the
heroes of the day.

Each group was a hermetic community defined by the
exclusive and difficult and dangerous skills its members possessed.

Why do I add the movie director to this group?

Like the others, his profession is romantic (i.e., it attracts
great common desire to be admitted and, once admitted, to
be successful within) until its technology is superseded. The
airline pilot becomes the driver with the appearance of the
astronaut. The canal boater is out of a job when the railroads
are built.

Motion pictures, again, stand on the cusp of the past and
the future. They draw on existing arts and combine them
into a legitimately new art. They are made to be shown in
a theater so that members of the audience can commune
with each other. To order the dreams of the populace so that

the populace en masse, acting as "the audience," can cele-brate itself, is the art of the movies.

The purpose of video is to hypnotize, to lull, to render "information" superior to suggestion and celebration.

It is no accident that the hero of video is not the pilot of the "entertainment," the director, but the pilot of technology, the "producer," the promoter, the packager.

The movies are a momentary and beautiful aberration of a technological society in the last stages of decay.

Their beauty resides in this: that they are actual records of the light which shone on us. Not only were they created to represent our dreams in this most troubled of times, but they were created to have the potential to live after us.

After the tapes have been erased, after the technology to retrieve them has been lost, someone, quite a while from now, might possibly just find a strip of film and hold it up to the light.

POLL FINDS

The name of Poet was almost forgotten, that of Orator was usurped by the sophists. A cloud of critics, of compilers, of commentators, darkened the face of learning, and the decline of genius was soon followed by the corruption of taste.

> Edward Gibbon,
> *The Decline and Fall of the Roman Empire*

 In *The New York Times* of March 1, 1989, we find an article on Richard M. Daley's victory in the Mayoral primary. We were informed that "the racial voting pattern was demonstrated by a *New York Times*, WBBM-TV poll of 2114 voters." Further, we were told in a sidebar that "in addition to sampling error, the practical difficulties of conducting any survey of voter opinion on primary election day may introduce other sources of error into the poll."

This disclaimer is a lot of small print to have to swallow. Are we, one might ask, or are we not dealing with a sure-fire barometer of public opinion? Would it not be a cruel irony if, having discarded that method of election prescribed by the Constitution, i.e., *voting*, for a less democratic but more scientific mechanism, polling, we were to find that we have sacrificed in vain?

We know that polls are inaccurate and unjust. We are drawn to them not because of their ability to predict the future, but because of their ability to relieve us of the responsibility for individual thought.

In subscribing to the poll's power "to do good," we choose to be relieved of uncertainty and assert ourselves ready to make this bargain: to happily live with the results of a stupid or incorrect decision if only we can avoid the responsibility for having made it.

The prevalence of polling in all facets of our daily life is a reversion to Mob Rule.

When an individual in power bases a decision on a survey, he or she becomes a demagogue, and derives power from an appeal to the emotions of the majority, specifically, the burning desire of the individual (subsumed in the majority) to be Right.

This demagogue abjures any notion of responsible action, and exchanges honor for continued employment.

In entertainment, in marketing, in politics, in medicine, in all areas of life, it is the momentary opinion of the majority which now determines the course of action.

Well, one might say, are the wishes of the majority to be overlooked? Isn't the jury process itself, to which we entrust the life and liberty of accused citizens, a poll? Yes. But it is a poll of individuals who have sworn to put aside prejudice, and judge facts impartially so as to serve the community-at-large.

The oath is designed to transform what would be a poll of the mob into a panel of dedicated citizens.

For the most vicious aspect of a poll is that it submerges the individual's responsibility for choice. The person who administers the poll has no responsibility, he or she sees the job as a gathering of impartial facts; the person who answers the poll has no responsibility; they are asked how they feel at any given moment, and the very inducement to answer is this: you will have no responsibility for how these statistics are used: you are free, you are, in fact, *encouraged* to answer as self-interestedly as you wish: for a moment there are no restrictions on your libido.

There are movies, plays, books, television shows the meaning and the worth of which can only be gauged over time and by reflection. It would be bad enough if the individual, on having seen these entertainments, were robbed of the capacity to reflect at leisure by questioning as to: how did you like, and would you recommend, and what aspect did you like best about the work. How much more dreadful it is that this information is used to create, to jury-rig works of pseudo-art, demagogical works whose only purpose is to grant power to their purveyors by appealing to the lowest emotion of the Masses.

For it is very difficult to tell *what one thinks* about a work of art immediately after having experienced it. There are works which one acclaims to the sky, and has forgotten the next day; there are, and we have all had this experience, works which we, on first acquaintance, adjudged unimportant, which have stayed with us literally all our lives.

Polling of the electorate appeals to our universal love of being right, and our universal love of being pandered to.

We have, and very well *may*, on reflection, endorse that candidate who calls our attention to hard truths, who calls our attention to the fact that we have been wrong in our action or direction, and that correction, though necessary, will be painful; we are, however, not so likely to endorse that candidate *without* reflection. And, in the heat of the moment, and immediately after having been appealed to as the Omnipotent Electorate, the True, or Old-fashioned, or Right-as-Rain American Voter, we are likely to adopt the demagogue's suggestion that we laugh to scorn anyone who tells us that we could possibly be in the wrong.

As is the case with entertainment, this poll of our lowest emotions is unfortunate enough, but even more so is the fact that these polls are used to calculate policy (which policy is always increasingly bald demagoguery), and to choose candidates (such candidates being chosen as is the policy).

Further, as polling has replaced voting as the method of electing our officials, our capacity to stand alone, to think alone, *to be content while being thought in the wrong* has all but evaporated. Faced with the poll which tells us our candidate *has no chance*, it is regrettable in the extreme, but most understandable that we choose not to vote, or to vote for the "winner"; and if the candidate is anything more than his or her television personality, if the candidate is, in fact, the platform for which he or she stands, and if, having, through reflection, chosen to endorse that platform, as it reflects our understanding of the nature of the world, our acceptance of the poll is our *rejection of our own thoughts or*

ideas because to hold them in opposition to "majority opinion" is not as important as to be thought "right." And there
we have American Fascism, in which we become our own
dictator, and have forced on ourselves the will, not of others,
but of the lowest aspect of ourselves; and this slavery has been
forced on us not by the threat of death or torture, but by the
threat of the momentary discomfort of being thought wrong.

In newspapers a growing majority of Page One stories are
headed "poll finds" and, almost universally, the finding of
the poll is either obvious, "Poll finds mental attitude can
help avert disease," and banality passes for news; or it is a
reflection, again, of the desire of the human being to have
low wishes fulfilled.

The secondary cost of this newspaper polling is the desire
of the Public, having expressed itself, to see its wish made
fact. For example, a headline of July 11th, 1987, from *The
New York Times*: POLL FINDS NORTH IS TELLING THE TRUTH.

What *can* a poll "find"?

There are two closely allied applicable meanings of "find."
One is "discovers."

What *can* a poll discover? Can it discover the truth? No,
it can, of course, only discover what several people *believe*
to be the truth. (If we believe in the methodology of the
Pollsters, and finally, why *should* we? Would we not be wiser
to presume that, as their masters have risen to power pan-
dering to the Masses under a false flag of statistical impar-
tiality, they will choose to thrive by bending statistics to serve
the will of their masters?) A poll, again, can only discover
what the polled believe *at that instant* to be true. A poll
cannot discover how many wives Henry VIII had.

The difference between what many people believe to be true and what may, in fact, *be* true is often and perhaps *most* times vast. And one of the organs created by Society for bringing public mood and actual fact into alignment is the newspaper. News organs which publish polls as news are content to thrive on a construction not a whit more elegant or laudable than this: "I dunno. A lot of people think it's true."

A second meaning for "finds," hidden in the *North* headline, and, by extension, wherever one sees the phrase *Poll Finds*, is "rules." And this is, I think, closer to the unfortunate truth of the phrase.

For when an organ of information effectually makes a ruling—each time it publishes a statistic of mood in a situation of dispute, it not only disregards its responsibility to inform, it corrupts by example.

Colonel North is in the process of being granted a *de facto* pardon. He is being excused from trial through extraordinary means, finally, because of the Will of the People as determined by the Poll. (For, if the Administration had "found" through perusal of polls, that public sentiment wanted North tried for the crimes of which he stands accused, he would, would he not, have stood trial in a real sense? And here we see the poll usurping not only the function of the Executive, but of the Judiciary.

We tend to Ask All Our Friends, that is to say, we tend to rely on statistics, when we are very confused. The issue of Colonel North, like many issues in our times, is very confusing.

Unfortunately, it, *like* many issues in our time, cannot be resolved by asking other people what they think.

In a time of National Confusion, our need for *example* is great.

Examples of calm, reasoned, responsible method and judgment will do much to promote like qualities in the public. Examples of demagoguery will do the same.

BLACK AS THE
ACE OF SPADES

They say you could take a bunch of men and put them in a room around a table with a pack of playing cards, but you can't induce them to pick up those cards unless they're betting on them. And if they're betting on them, they can sit for hours or for days.

And you can take those same men sitting at a table, but even the reward of money to be won is not enough inducement to those men to push that money back and forth for hours unless they also happen to be holding cards.

So it's not just the money, and it's not just the cards. But you put the two together and a magic is created.

The game is not about money. The game is about love, and divine intervention. The money is a propitiatory gift to the Gods. It is the equivalent of Fasting and Prayer: it is to gain the God's attention, and to put the supplicant in the properly humbled frame of mind to receive any information which might be forthcoming.

For the Cards are the symbols of the universe. There are few of them, but their possible combinations are myriad.

We have favorites, and intelligence informs us that we will be rewarded not by fealty to symbols, but only by our correct understanding of combinations. And yet, we have favorites.

There are good luck cards and bad luck cards. Pushkin writes about the Queen of Spades; the Ace of Spades has been called the Death Card (I am a native of Chicago, and in that city, and in various other cities where I have played, that ace was called "Chicago"), and in American Folklore, the Jack of Diamonds is a trouble card and is known as Jack the Bear. I have my own Good Luck cards, but I would not tax my luck by naming them.

When we are betting on the cards, we love their combinations. Their beautiful unfolding means that God Loves Us, their malevolent conjunction means that Someone is Trying to Teach Us a Lesson.

Cardplayers dream of cards. We have a saying, "A winner can't get enough to eat, and a loser can't sleep." I have dreamed of cards, and there are hands that I remember twenty years later—hands that I know I will never forget.

I've also had a recurring dream. I have it once or twice a year: I am playing poker and have been dealt a magnificent hand, a leadpipe cinch (which is to say "a certain winner"). As I am about to lay down my hand and claim the pot, I discover that I have one too many cards in my hand, and that, through no fault of my own, my hand is now invalid. I finally succeed in discarding the unwanted card, and then find that I now have two too many cards in my hand, et cetera.

Such powerful symbols.

Playing cards are a survival of our less rational, more frightful, more beautiful past. They commemorate a numerology based on thirteen rather than ten; they restate the mythological hierarchy of Monarchy, of a state which recapitulates our infant understanding of the family-as-world; they suggest and are employed for gambling—one of the two forbidden or curtailed pastimes in the repressed, rational civilization. The cards may be diverting, or dangerous, or destructive. They are never neutral.

KRYPTONITE

A PSYCHOLOGICAL APPRECIATION

 I was back in my child-
hood home of Chi-
cago. I'd come back to
celebrate Passover at my Father's House, which I hadn't done
in twenty years.

I took a long walk down the Lakefront, along the various
parks and beaches where I'd played as a boy. I tasted the
Chicago Park District water out of the stone birdbath drinking
fountains, and it tasted the same as it had those many years
ago when it was not only cold and delicious, but also forbidden—we were in the midst of the Polio scare—and my
mother grudgingly allowed us to go play in the park, but
made us swear that we would not drink out of the fountains
and so risk contagion. I ended my walk on Oak Street Beach.
I sat down on the stone ledge and watched a group of boys

skateboarding. They'd made a plywood ramp, and they took turns running up to it on their skateboards, and jumping over it, performing various feats while in the air.

It was quite beautiful, and as I was in a sentimental mood, it, too, took me back to my boyhood.

I remembered what it was like to be a boy, and to turn a simple, rather meaningless act into a skill through constant and endless repetition. I remembered throwing rocks at a streetlamp on summer evenings, my friends and I, for hours and hours. I remembered throwing a beachball up out of sight onto the garage roof and making the most intricate game out of judging where it would land.

I remembered bike chases, a sort of capture-the-flag/ring-a-levio, games which lasted all night.

As I sat watching the skateboards, a bicyclist passed in front of me. He had a bicyclelock, tradename *Kryptonite*, affixed to his bike.

And I thought it a nice American in-joke, that his bicyclelock was named after an artifact from the Superman comics.

I enjoyed the Superman comics as a boy.

I enjoyed their very dullness and predictability. The story never varied and, even as a child, I remembered thinking, "What a dull fantasy."

But I enjoyed them. And the story that I enjoyed was this: Superman is engaged in doing good. Playing on his desire to do good, the Evildoers lure him into a dangerous situation, and he is exposed by them to Kryptonite, a fragment of the now-destroyed world on which Superman was born. Kryptonite is the only substance in the world capable of harming

Superman, and he now begins to die. At the last possible moment, he is rescued from the Kryptonite by some happy chance, and the cycle may now begin again.

As I mulled over the story, I thought, "Why is the bikelock named *Kryptonite?*" It was named *Kryptonite* because it is to be thought of as strong, as invincible.

But, I thought, Kryptonite is strong only to one end: to destroy. And, as I so thought, a deeper meaning of the Superman story occurred to me.

Superman is born on the planet Krypton. Krypton is near destruction, and Superman's beloved father, Jor-El, uses his last moments of life to put his son in a rocket and fire him to earth.

On Earth, the child is adopted and raised by a kindly, if somewhat distant, Ma and Pa Kent.

As their adopted son, Clark Kent, the child moves to the big city, Metropolis, where he takes a job at the *Daily Planet* newspaper. When Goodness is threatened in Metropolis, the man transforms himself from Clark Kent, who is portrayed as an innocuous and fairly unattractive man, into Superman, in which guise he wins the awe and adulation of the Populace. After righting the wrongs of Metropolis, however, he must flee from the populace, and the pleasures they might award him, and change himself back into Clark Kent. Why must he flee? Because of the presence of Kryptonite. If his archenemies knew of his whereabouts, they would be free to seek him out and secretly introduce Kryptonite into his presence, and he would die.

His power is obtained, then, at the expense of any possibility of personal pleasure.

As Clark Kent, he is in love with his co-worker, the reporter Lois Lane. She finds the attentions of Kent, the milquetoast, laughable. She is in love with Superman. Superman cannot reciprocate. *He cannot tell her his secret, for to do so would imperil his life.* He can tell *no one* his secret. He can have adulation without intimacy, or he may long for intimacy with no hope of reciprocation.

Superman comics are a fable, not of strength, but of disintegration. They appeal to the preadolescent mind not because they reiterate grandiose delusions, but because they reiterate a very deep cry for help.

Superman's two personalities can be integrated only in one thing: only in death. Only Kryptonite cuts through the disguises of wimp and hero, and affects the man below the disguises.

And what is Kryptonite? Kryptonite is all that remains of his childhood home.

It is the remnants of that destroyed childhood home, and the fear of those remnants, which rule Superman's life. The possibility that the shards of that destroyed home might surface prevents him from being intimate—they prevent him from sharing the knowledge that the wimp and the hero are one. The fear of his childhood home prevents him from having pleasure.

He fears that to reveal his weakness, and confusion, is, perhaps indirectly, but certainly inevitably, to receive death from the person who received that information.

Superman fears women. All of his love interests are given the initials L.L.: Lois Lane, Lori Lemaris, Lana Lang; and it is not coincidental that his arch-enemy, the super fiend of all his most harrowing adventures, is named, similarly, Lex Luthor.

Superman fears women and withholds himself sexually. He presents to the world two false fronts: one of *impotence*, and the other of *benevolence*, both disguises created to protect him from Woman's fury—fury at *what* we cannot know, but fury it certainly is—for he says as clear as day, to Lois Lane: you would not take me when I was weak (Kent) and you cannot have me when I am strong.

Several years ago a book was done commemorating Fifty Years of Superman Comics. And I was asked, along with many other writers, to contribute a quote. I said that I admired Superman: I admire anyone who can make his living in his underwear. And the hero aspect of the fantasy: the fantasy of *omnipotence* has, indeed, echoes of the psychology of someone who spends his life in his underwear: of the psychology of the infant.

Superman is stuck in the loop of the attempt to master-through-repetition: he has put himself back in infancy, and is playing out this dream/wish: "I do nothing but good. I ask nothing for myself. In fact, I *can take* nothing for myself. Perhaps if I do enough good my world will not be destroyed, and I will not be sent away from home."

Far from being invulnerable, Superman is the most vulnerable of beings, because his childhood was destroyed. He can never reintegrate himself by returning to that home—it is gone. It is gone and he is living among aliens to whom he cannot even reveal his rightful name.

There is no hope for him but constant hiding, and prayer that his enemies will not learn his true identity. No amount of good works can protect him.

He has not only relinquished any claim on citizenship, he has relinquished any hope of sexual manhood, of intimacy, of peace. "I do good but take no pleasure," he says, "I ask nothing for myself. I pray that my false-self attracts no notice: forget about me."